Chapter One

"So all the generations from Abraham to David are 14
generations; and from David until the carrying away into
Babylon are 14 generations; and from the carrying away
into Babylon unto Christ are 14 generations."
(2 Kings 24:14, Mathew 1:17)

Machaerus, Adar (Feb) 29 AD

Decius Invictus squinted at the noonday glare of Adar's winter sun glittering off the
monotonous desert. Palestine's boulders mirrored identical tan tones in every tower and edifice
of the Machaerus castle. The opposite direction across the Mediterranean, his Italian home with
its bountiful shades of green called to him. For 20 years he foolishly considered Rome's marble
structures commonplace, now he missed their stately lines set against the emerald shades of the
world's boundless sun.

Decius entered his charge's chambers. The normally argumentative tones of Salome and
her maid, Ide, had turned to screams, summoning his presence. A full rainbow of swirling colors
momentarily blinded and confused him. Purple and red curtains billowed into the room from the
columned terrace. Salome's yellow and white bed hangings were being torn from their upper
moorings. Striped zebra hides moved across the slick marble floor with a bevy of puppies
tugging and rolling about. Decius noted one white pup lying too still on the tiles next to the door.

On the bed Salome's long red tunic was hiked up past her knees. Her auburn hair splayed across the yellow silk coverlet. Even her maid's black braids were coming unbound by the girls' violent thrashings about. Ide's blue-gray garment was twisted under Salome's legs. They continued to wrestle, immodest in their anger.

Salome wrapped a yellow strip of bed hanging around Ide's neck. She tightened her grip, screaming, "I'll kill you. You murdered my puppy. You worthless animal."

Luckily, the drapery pulled away from the bed's upper frame as Ide struggled against her mistress's hands.

Decius picked Salome up from the bed, stilled her flailing arms against his breastplate of leather braces. "Princess, think of what havoc you are wreaking."

He nearly swooned from the rose perfume washing over his senses from Salome's hair and her heated limbs. Decius opened his mouth to draw sufficient air into his struggling lungs. His eyes closed as he briefly relished Salome's closeness.

"What?" Herodias boomed out her reproach as she entered the chambers. "Unhand my daughter!"

Decius dutifully dropped his arms.

Salome rushed to escape, but her hair caught in the lacings of his chest armor.

"Wait," he called, trying not to harm his mistress. He reached out, stopping her. "Your hair."

Salome's imperial mother approached. "Ide, come to your senses. Hand me your knife." The frightened, coughing girl righted herself from the floor. She approached cautiously with her personal weapon drawn. Herodias snatched the knife and quickly severed the caught strands of her daughter's hair from Decius's buckles. "Explain yourself."

Decius bowed, going down to one knee. "Your majesty." He welcomed the steadying effect of the cool marble beneath his knee. He did not dare raise his eyes.

Salome explained, "Ide dropped my favorite puppy. He's dead and I want her slain, too."

Decius could see the white dog without raising his head.

"Stand," Herodias ordered. "Carry out your mistress's orders."

Decius drew his sword and approached the cowering maid. As he raised the sharp blade, he prayed his war experience would allow Ide a quick death.

But Salome leapt up and grabbed his arm, nearly causing him to slice away half of Ide's face; instead, the blade cut off a wide swathe of Ide's braided hair.

"Mother, I'm sorry," Salome pleaded. "Please, Decius, sheath your weapon."

Herodias dismissed the incident. "Salome, you need to dress for Herod's dinner. Ide, I'll attend to you when I have time. Scoop up these animals, Decius. In the future, do not take liberties with your mistress's person."

"Yes, your majesty." Decius swept the puppies into one of the rugs and hefted the bundle over his shoulder, thankful for his reprieve. But his body didn't feel immediate release. His nostrils still held the rose scent from Salome's hair.

After depositing the animals in an empty stall in the stables, Decius unknotted the strands of Salome's hair from his buckles. Determined to cherish these mementoes of her closeness, he held them to his nose as he walked back to his post outside Salome's chambers. Would he ever be able to hold her in his arms, again? Next time he wanted her to be a willing participant in the pleasure he had experienced.

Leaning against the warm wall of the outer hall to Salome's rooms, Decius closed his eyes, reached for his usual calm state of alertness. The future held little promise of the princess even remembering which of the palace guards had restrained her. He was thankful that Salome

stayed Ide's execution. Her upset over the dropped puppy was understandable, the life-and-death

power of her position schooled her to denounce Ide. Salome's family history of regal death

decrees had set a heady precedence for a 14-year-old girl's righteous anger.

Just then, Salome entered the outer portico with a burden wrapped in white satin similar

to the strip she had strangled Ide with. She held the dead puppy at arms length.

Decius bowed and accepted the puppy. "I'll bury her facing Rome, my lady."

Salome's great green eyes sparkled with tears held at bay with royal restraint. "Facing

east toward the Lord's coming will do, Decius." She re-entered her rooms.

Decius blinked, realizing he would remain at Salome's service all his life. He had

breathed her essence into his life's blood. Hearing his name from her mouth in her own sweet

tones convinced him he could now mourn those old, shady streets of Rome.

At 20 years of age, after the death of his parents from a plague, the pull of foreign lands

had encouraged him to volunteer for duty with Pontius Pilate's occupation forces. Now, the rest

of his life would be spent in this bleak colorless land, living within earshot of Salome's beck-

and-call to provide sufficient sustenance.

Movement on the road leading north to the Sea of Galilee drew his attention. Along the

desolate eastern shore of the Dead Sea, a steady stream of the ragged disciples of John-the

Baptist continued to approach. The prophet's confinement in Machaerus castle's prison failed to

diminish his reputation. These travelers would also camp near the grate of John's basement cell.

Decius was entranced by their loyalty. The ancient lyricism of the Hebrew language made

it easy for Decius to memorize. He had imagined the beauty of its careful translation would

trigger a poetic resurgence in Rome. When his duties were not required after the evening

changing of the guard, Decius often found himself among the prophet's audience, studying the
nuances of the language while spellbound by its prophetic content.

John the Baptist was *not* averse to repetition. He often spoke of the Messiah's baptism in
Bethabara beyond the Jordan. John's disciples had also been baptizing in Aenon near to Salim
with Jesus's disciples. Decius heard John's disciples ask him, "Rabbi, He that was with thee
beyond Jordan, to whom thou barest witness, the same baptizeth, and all men come to Him."

John answered and said, "A man can receive nothing, except it be given him from
heaven. Ye yourselves bear me witness, that I said, 'I am not the Christ, but that I am sent before
Him. He that believeth on the Son hath everlasting life: and he that believeth not the Son shall
not see life; but the wrath of God abideth on him."

Decius recited the prophet's words to himself, careful to remember each intonation and
correct ending of each word.

Tetrarch Herod was too frightened of John-the-Baptist's powers to issue any order to
disperse his followers. Although he knew that Herod listened as avidly as anyone, Decius was
surprised at the number of publicans, Pharisees and Sadducees who made the long trip to
Machaerus to hear the prophet's words each day. The Baptist had raised his normally quiet voice
to shout at them from his echoing basement prison. "O generation of vipers, who hath warned
you to flee from the wrath to come?"

Decius doubted Salome knew the often-repeated phrases of the Baptist, but she had told
him to plant the dead puppy facing east toward the Lord's coming. If he could summon the
courage, he would ask her if she knew John's main message. "I indeed baptize you with water
unto repentance; but He that cometh after me is mightier than I. Repent: for the kingdom of
heaven is at hand."

Salome's mother, Herodias, found reason to fear and hate the prophet. She had divorced her first husband, Philip; but Jewish law had forbidden her to her to marry his brother, Herod, causing the holy man to decry her wickedness whenever he listed the sins of the nation and its occupiers.

Decius wished he could kidnap Salome away from the horrors of her stepfather's royal court. But where could he spirit her away to? The high plateau Machaerus was perched on provided a view in all four directions. Only night would allow escape. Decius knew he could keep on the northern path to Galilee at night, but the southern route to Jerusalem would less likely be searched. The southern road around the Dead Sea was nearly unknown to Decius. He could correct that situation, planning to place markers along the path to lead them through the darkness. How much time would he need? At least the days were fairly short in the winter month of Adar. As soon as the sun set, he would lay out their path for some future flight. Four hours by horse should allow enough time to find a hiding place near the Sea's southern shore.

Decius dug a deep grave for Salome's puppy. He unwrapped the lifeless animal from its swaddling, cutting the shiny white satin into flags to mark an escape route for Salome and himself.

*   *   *

Salome had not minded being restrained in the strong arms of Decius Invictus. He hadn't harmed her and had even saved her from having her hair torn out by the roots. He seemed pleased that she stopped him from killing Ide. His slight smile showed his approval. Salome examined the severed ends of part of her tresses.

Ide interrupted her reverie. "Please, mistress, I'll take care of your hair later. You need to dress."

When Salome had handed Decius the swaddled dead pup, Decius's blue eyes steadied as he promised to bury her dear pet. She trusted him with the task. She wondered where the remaining puppies were now. Salome rubbed her arms, remembering his heated touch when he had restrained her from strangling Ide.

"Princess, please raise your arms." Ide tried to lift Salome's red chemise above her head.

"Where is the dress Mother wants me to dance in?" Salome waited as Ide brought the dress out from behind the alabaster-and-gold dressing screen.

"Isn't it marvelous?"

Salome's critical gaze surveyed the monstrosity. "It must weigh ten mina with all the gold cords weaving down those green pleats."

"These aren't pleats. Watch." Ide made the dress swirl around. "They're slits, so that Tetrarch Herod can see your form the better. The green silk will enhance the color of your eyes."

"What do I wear under it?" The gold strands were prickly, almost barbs. A cold frisson slid down Salome's spine. What was her mother up to now? Accumulation of gold was Herodias's main occupation and the constant activity of hoarding more and more gold was her mother's only goal as far as Salome could determine. Leaving her father, Philip, was motivated by the wealth in Herod's territories. Philip's Tetrarch was poorer than the grand temples in the provinces in Herod's region around Jerusalem. The Emperor Tiberius understood, too. He had sanctioned Herodias's divorce, which went against Jewish law.

And Tiberius ruled.

The prophet in prison beneath them had spoken too openly about her mother's break with the law. Herodias didn't have the patience to wait for Salome's father to die and even Tiberius would have been suspicious of Philip's death by food poisoning. Salome wondered how long the prophet would survive.

Ide brought over an undergarment, the short black silk chemise tied above one shoulder. As Salome allowed Ide to dress her, she recalled her studious father's less ostentatious home. Against Jewish tradition, he had taught his only child, a sorry girl, to read Hebrew. Salome loved their time together reading the scrolls. Salome was awarded the priceless gift of the 23rd Psalm. As she had promised her father, she recited the beautiful prayer morning and evening.

David had danced before the Ark of the Covenant. To Salome dancing was the same expression of the joy of life, a prayer of thankfulness. The lurid hints from the old king's harem escaped Salome. Only the harp, flute and zither prompted Salome's limbs to leap and sway to the melodies. "At least I'll be decent while I'm dancing."

"For a while," Ide cautioned.

"Who is attending the dinner?" Salome's position at court rarely caused jitters.

"Only the highest ranked captains in Pilate's troops, the owners of the biggest estates in Herod's domain and the territorial tribal Lords. The oldest Flavius Josephus. Did you know his father plans to name all his sons, Flavius? The guests are already assembling in the banquet hall." Ide began to dress Salome's hair with bells and green jade. "Your mother thinks you will be fit entertainment."

"Aren't the other girls dancing?" Salome counted off the youngest members of the old King Herod's harem. Twelve adolescent women practiced daily for the month prior to Herod's birthday celebration. They imitated the older dancers' movements. Salome hadn't joined the juvenile dancers' derisive laughter at their elders' stiffness in their backbends and somersaults.

"They'll all be wearing black," Ide confided, "so as not to detract from this dress. I heard Herodias direct them to encircle you and then turn their backs at the end."

"Will they stop dancing?" Salome twisted her head back and forth pleased with the music caused by the bells in her whirling hair.

"They'll shield you from the other diners." Ide placed castanets on Salome's ankles and wrists. "Only Herod will see your entire dance."

Salome experienced no relief to hear this bit of news. As she let Ide apply rose-scented ointment to her arms, neck, and thighs, she wondered if Decius Invictus would be present with the other household guards. Would he enjoy her dance; or, would he be embarrassed by her mother's plan to seduce Herod into giving more golden treasures to Herodias?

*   *   *

As soon as the sun disappeared in red glory, Decius rode south. He placed the white flags under appropriately heavy stones along the southern escape route. His presence wouldn't be missed for the hours when the horde of hungry guests gorged themselves. Would Salome need to escape with him tonight? Decius was well prepared. On his return to the prison-castle, Decius counted off the satin markers shimmering in the moonlight. He scanned the sky to see if clouds threatened to stop the night's moon-glow.

Circling Machaerus, Decius assumed his usual position among the crowd and disciples listening to jailed John the Baptist.

Decius was not the only house staff to seek out the prophet's wisdom each night. The youngest of the Roman guards asked the prophet, "What must we do?"

John the Baptist's voice was loud enough for them all to hear, "Do not bear false witness, do not ask for higher wages, and do not lie."

Decius was struck by the ramifications of these three simple rules. Their wages were a heavy burden on the occupied Jewish people. Taxes ate up nearly three-quarters of every household's income. Herod's father had gathered funds to build the city of Tiberius on the Jewish graveyard at the southeastern shore of the Sea of Galilee. The port city of Caesarea, as well as the renovations to the castle in the walled city of Jerusalem meant more taxes on the inhabitants. Stadiums and temples were built in all the new towns to show the present Tetrarch Herod's obeisance to Rome.

Most of the guards supplemented their pay by witnessing in court against the citizens of the land. If the accused didn't have enough money to pay for lies, then the soldiers could always be assured the taxation judges would hand out a few shekels to weigh down justice.

In carrying out the outlandish commands of the Tetrarch's household, inevitable falsehoods diminished the instances of life-and-death encounters with one despot or another. To survive one had to become adept in giving the desired answer to every question. Truth fled.

These three rules from the prophet might sound artless enough; however, the words were revolutionary dictates to the keepers of the unsteady peace in Palestine. Decius wondered if John-the-Baptist's disciples knew how dangerous the man they had followed into the wilderness really was. They might soon find out. Prison was only the beginning of the prophet's fate.

A heavy feeling of dread made Decius search the sky for approaching storms. The bright stars blinked at his fears. He could hear the musicians increasing the pace of the dances on the rooftop-dining hall as he returned to the castle. Salome's dance troupe was entertaining the guests for Herod's birthday.

As Decius Invictus approached the banquet hall, the bright torches, the constantly increasing din of music and raised voices, and the vying aromas of the different dinner dishes, failed to diminish his overwhelming sense of approaching doom.

Decius arrived in the midst of Salome's dance. Herod and Herodias sat side-by-side, sharing dishes of fruit, marinated fish and sweetened breads on the table behind their reclining couches. Herodias hair was piled high to display as many jewels in her possession as possible. Herod's rich robe lay open exposing his hairy, stumpy legs.

Perpendicular to the royal couple's raised seating, two long tables held the dignitaries of the region, decked out in their finest robes. Servants laden with heavy trays of delicacies and dressed meats bustled about to keep up with the guests' rate of emptying plates and goblets. All eyes of the visitors were fixed on the dancers' movements.

Salome's dress of green and gold highlighted the red splendor of her hair. The other dancers were of no interest to Decius. Salome's long hair swept her shoulders, falling to her waist. The green glass beads and tinkling bells tied to her hair accentuated her movements. Her hands swaying gracefully above her head, lost in the melody, responding to its promptings in perfect rhythm with the castanets on her wrists and ankles, Salome seemed oblivious of her powerful female charms.

*   *   *

Salome whirled to the increasing tempo of the musicians, focusing on the faces of

Herodias and Herod to check her dizziness. Salome once smiled at the furrowed brow of Decius

Invictus. His worried look instantly changed the happy mood of her dance.

The faces of her stepfather and mother began to resemble each other. Her mother wore no

beard, but she had raised a black napkin to her red lips, which mimicked the wine-bloated leer

above Herod's black beard.

Salome stopped.

Her mother beckoned with her black napkin, offering her sweet brandy to quench her

thirst. After Salome drank the fiery liquor, she reached for the beaker of water that Ide held out

for her. Salome swallowed the cool liquid ridding her mouth of the heady liquor.

Herod bellowed, startling the other men at the side tables. "Dance! Ask for anything, up

to half my kingdom!"

Herodias drew Salome to her, loosening the tie on her black chemise. "When you finish,

ask for John-the-Baptist's head on a charger."

Salome nearly stumbled toward the raised dance floor. Her dizziness wasn't caused by the

dance steps. Her head was spinning from the liquor even as she stood absolutely still. The

chemise slipped to the floor.

The musicians were quick to restart another dance, slower than the first. Salome swayed

to the music, forgetting how scantily clothed she was under the pleated dress. She nearly

stumbled as she stepped out of the fallen chemise.

Herodias smiled but Salome noticed her eyes were cold, calculating each of her

daughter's moves. Nonplussed and then horrified, Salome understood. Her mother was selling

her to Herod for whatever pleasure he could glean, for whatever price he would pay.

Herod's eyes were heated with lust. He licked his foul lips.

As Salome swung around in the dance, the dress twirled out from her hips. Aware of her mother's wickedness, Salome stopped again, but the gold cords of the dress lashed and cut her bared knees. She spun to keep the dress from tearing at her legs.

Herodias's smile widened. The hatred in her eyes was obvious now. Herodias was enjoying the pain the dress was inflicting on her daughter as her husband's exhilaration increased. The music became louder. Salome lost track of time. Her mother hated her. Salome heard her breaking heart pounding in her ears. She raised her hands to stop the noise and noticed they were bloodied. The wetness running down her legs and making the marble floor slick was her own blood. Salome collapsed on the floor to keep the dreaded golden lashes from injuring her further.

Herod approached and knelt down, his heated breath near her ear. "What did she tell you to ask for?"

Salome responded in truth, "Bring the head of John the Baptist on a charger."

Herod stood as if suddenly aware of their audience. Nevertheless, he waved to the guards to carry out Herodias's order.

Herodias came to her daughter's aid, triumphantly offering her the black chemise. When Ide wound the dress around Salome's legs, the maid's arms became bloodied, too. Still lying prone on the blood-strewn floor, Salome searched for Decius, but couldn't find him.

Herod and all the guests, except her mother, had escaped from the nightmarish outcome of Salome's dance. Salome imagined she could hear the stomp of the guards as they approached from the basement prison.

One guard laid the severed head at Salome's feet, before he and his cohorts fled. Salome knelt to raise the offering to her insane mother. Herodias claimed the silver plate, walked to an open portal and threw it out into the darkness.

Salome fainted into Ide's arms.

Chapter Two

"It is written, 'Man shall not live by bread alone, but
by every word that proceedeth out of the mouth of
God.'"

(Deut. 8:3; Matt. 4:4)

Decius returned to the recently abandoned banquet hall. At first, he knelt next to Ide, who was desperately trying to tend to her unconscious mistress. Then, Decius stood and commandeered three skins of wine and an untouched basket of bread from the tables. He ripped all the tablecloths out from under the serving dishes. Tearing one cloth in half, he tucked its fold into his belt. "Ide," he directed softly, "use your knife to cut this fabric into strips. Cleanse her wounds in wine before you wrap them. If she wakes, give her wine. No one will bother you here. I'll return."

"I need to wash her hair." Ide whimpered, struggling to untie the bells from Salome's tangles.

"She'll need a disguise to survive, now." Decius wept at the sight of his proud, young mistress reduced to a pile of golden litter, bloodied and spent limbs. "Cut her hair off." Decius stifled another sob. "It will grow back. Replace the dance dress with your top robe."

"What about all this gold?" Ide peeled a strip of gold from the lascivious dress.

"Coil the gold strips inside the bread basket and then replace the bread." Decius rushed to the open archway. "Don't leave her side for a moment."

"Never," Ide promised.

Decius grabbed a torch from the wall and ran down the path from Machaerus, down to the floor of the desert to search for the severed head of John the Baptist. He located the correct portico from which Herodias had pitched the charger from the rooftop. Holding the torch high, he wondered if he should call the other disciples to help. First, he saw the glint of silver then he spied what looked like a wooly rock. He draped the white tablecloth over the suspected mound; the material instantly darkened with blood.

Hearing the moans of the disciples near John's cell, Decius joined them. The guards had let them plead to Herod for John's body. The Tetrarch had waved them away with what they concluded was permission. So far, they had constructed a litter with the partial body swaddled atop. Decius recognized Jacob, the cousin of John and brother of Jesus. He handed him the dreaded package.

Jacob accepted it without a word and placed it with the body, taking off his own robe to cover the corpse on the stretcher. Decius pulled at Jacob's seamless alb, sobbing so violently he was afraid his plea might not be understood. "Who, who will help a fa...fallen dancer?" He wanted to explain Salome's innocence but couldn't hope to be believed.

Jacob seized Decius's torch, held it high, for a better look at this weeping Roman guard of the household. "I know you. You've been with the audience of John."

"I've memorized all of John-the-Baptist's words." Decius knelt before the blessed disciple. "Who will help us now?"

"Tell me one phrase of John's and I will name a haven for your dancer." Jacob still held the torch high.

The other disciples stopped their keening to listen.

"Repent ye, for the kingdom of God is at hand." A certain calm overcame Decius from the remembered words, as if John or his good spirit was surrounding them. He stood, renewed in his search for a refuge for Salome.

Jacob placed a hand on Decius's shoulder, then whispered in his ear. "Mary, my mother and the mother of Jesus of Nazareth, is the only soul in all of Palestine who will take you in. Her house is near the gate to give comfort to travelers." Then clapping Decius on his chest, he added, "God's speed. We must leave now."

Decius hurried back to Machaerus. The darkened, emptied castle held a deadly quiet. He walked to where he had secured his team of horses to the largest, swiftest chariot. As he passed the stall where he had dropped the puppies, he reached in and grabbed one at random. The puppy was pure black. He tucked the pup into a bag of feed, next to a skin of water in the chariot. He brought his vehicle as close to the doorway of the royal chambers as possible. Then he ran up to the rooftop to rescue Salome.

Ide held the shorn Salome bundled in her arms next to an arch of the unlit, banquet hall. "She'll need me," she said.

"Of course," Decius decided Ide would be helpful, as he picked up Salome's light body and showed Ide where the chariot stood.

They packed Salome among the supplies of feed, flagons of wine and water and the heavy breadbasket into the three-wheeled chariot. Ide crouched and held her mistress's shorn head. Decius stepped in, lifted the reins and urged his team to leave Machaerus, forever.

*   *   *

Salome awoke to pain and jostling, which heightened each stab of awareness. She raised

her hand to her head. Finding no hair, she screamed. The chariot stopped. She felt Ide's hands on

her face.

"Mistress," Ide pleaded, "What can I do?"

Decius was there in the night, kneeling close to Salome. "Decius," she asked, "Why did

Mother cut my hair? Am I going to prison? Am I dying?"

"We're taking you to a safe haven, Mistress." The moonlight showed wet traces on

Decius cheeks. "Drink a little wine to ease your pain."

Then Salome remembered her dance, the horror of her mother…. Salome moaned. "No

one will house me now, Decius. I might as well be a leper."

"You are my mistress." Decius took her hand and placed it on the top of his thick curls,

dancing with silver highlights from the moon's glow. "Ide and I will take care of you. Quiet your

fears."

Salome removed her hand. "I cannot pay you."

Ide answered. "We're not with you for gain, Mistress. Decius and I both love you."

Their loyalty humbled her. "God protect us." Salome let herself slip back to sleep induced

by exhaustion and pain.

*   *   *

Decius moved the feed sack to protect Salome's body from the rough motion of the chariot.

Ide interrupted his ministrations. "We need to wash her wounds, soon."

"I know where there is a hidden cove at the tip of the Dead Sea," Decius whispered. "I planned to hide and feed the horses there. The salt sea will help cleanse any infection the sweetened wine might have caused."

"Thank heaven her face wasn't marked." Ide caressed Salome's cropped curls. "Why did you plan to hide your chariot?"

Decius hung his head. This serving girl already knew he wasn't being truthful. "Salome seemed destined to be victimized." He sighed, acknowledging the truth to himself. "I've planned to rescue her since I first laid eyes on her."

"To kidnap her." Ide held Salome closer, as if to protect her from his lurid designs. Ide's darker skin contrasted with the pale, delicate coloring of Salome.

"Only to serve her." Decius touched Ide's arm gently, so that she might see if not feel his sincerity.

Ide appeared mollified. "But how will we pass through the cities when it's daylight?"

Decius worried, too. How was he going to conceal them when the night could no longer keep them hidden in its folds? He drove his horses on; hoping their movement toward the cove would bring some further plan into his head. His emotions eased. He hoped his mind would provide some coherent thought, soon. Seeing the eastern sky brighten as dawn threatened, he prayed aloud, surprised at his attempt to believe. "Please let the God of Abraham protect this innocent."

When he found the inlet near the southern-most saltpans of Sedom, he reined in his team near the wall of an overhanging cliff. Decius carried Salome, as Ide spread out one of the tablecloths on the sand. He laid Salome down, careful not to wake the injured child. Then he whispered to Ide, "I'll purchase some male clothing and come back for you." Decius sized up the young girls. "Are you willing to cut your hair, too?"

Ide pulled on her braids. "Buy us caps, the round decorated ones that the harem boys wear. Hair is a lot of work. But then, you wouldn't appreciate that. Men only want beauty."

Decius defended himself. "We want peace, too."

He compared the fragile beauty of Salome's face to Ide's squared chin and thicker features. Salome's eyebrows above her closed green eyes were strawberry blonde whereas Ide's were black, bushy and nearly meeting across the bridge of her prominent nose. He was thankful for Ide's steady devotion to Salome. He worried about getting rid of his armor and the Roman chariot. "When I return, we'll need to travel with only a mule. Salome will ride the mule, but are you willing to walk all the way to Nazareth?"

"I will go wherever my mistress goes, for as long as she wants me to." Ide began cutting off her braids with her knife.

"Bury the hair, so it won't be found," Decius said, tapping the top of Ide's head. "What did you do with Salome's hair?"

"I threw her curls into the fireplace." Ide winced as she cut through another braid.

Decius realized the servant's full worth. "Your head is of more value to your mistress than your hair. Keep telling me your ideas for our escape."

Ide smiled for the first time since Decius became aware of her among Salome's many maids. "You might want to dress as an Egyptian with a turban to hide your crown of blond curls."

"I will," Decius said, feeling his mouth almost form a smile.

*   *   *

Salome awoke when Decius placed her body in the Dead Sea.

His strong arms cradled her safely. The heavily salted water let her float in a sitting position on the surface. As the salt permeated the dressings on her leg wounds the pain was excruciating.

Not wanting to scream like a child, Salome sought out Decius's hand and squeezed his thumb as hard as she could, until at last the pain overwhelmed her conscious mind.

*   *   *

\   "We've killed her," Ide whispered.

"She'll be all right." Decius hoped. "She's a strong young girl."

"Do people die from pain?" Ide helped him place Salome back on her bed under the sheltering overhang.

"Trust me, Ide." Decius turned his back. "Redress her wounds after the bandages are dry." He emptied the chariot of all their provisions. The black puppy stuck its head out of the feed sack. Decius handed the pup by the scruff of its neck to Ide. "Probably thirsty."

"Oh," Ide cooed to the miniature beast hugging it to her breast. "Salome will be pleased."

The sky lightened further with orange glowing clouds. "I'll return as soon as I can. Never leave her side."

Ide glared at him. "You already have my oath."

Decius dismounted the chariot and placed his hand under Ide's chin. "I've offended you, again. Please forgive me."

Ide stepped back as if struck. "A servant needs no apology."

"You are not a servant to Salome." Decius nodded his approval. "You are her only friend."

"And you?" Ide asked.

But Decius could not answer. He wanted to be more than a friend, more than a protector, more than anyone Salome had ever loved or thought of. He wanted to mean as much to her as she, her existence, every breath in her body meant to him. "She is my life," he said.

Ide acknowledged the fact with a nod.

*   *   *

Toward Bethlehem

Decius pushed the chariot off a nearby cliff into the Dead Sea. He watched hoping the heavy chariot would sink completely out of sight. He wondered if Ide or Salome had heard the splash from where he had left them. Salome's wounds were not serious. He imagined her flight into sleep could be her soul's way of protecting her from the realities of her mother's hatred. He busied his hands with re-harnessing his team into a string of pack animals.

The sun was well above the horizon when Decius found a sheep farmer's compound just outside of Bethlehem. After accepting water from the well for his team, Decius drank, too. He bartered for the sheepherder's mule for one horse, asking for one of the trained dogs to be thrown into the bargain, as an after thought.

The man, considered his feet. "I can't part with any of my dogs."

By the time the sly old man had agreed to give Decius his limping, ancient dog named 'Home,' there were only two horses left to trade. "Is there anyone you know in need of these draft animals?"

The herder was pleased to help, probably thinking a friend might profit by Decius's inability to barter. "My brother Aaron's compound is just over the hill. He told me last month that he plans to plant vegetables for the market. He'll need a team to plow the fields."

By noon, Decius had happily gained coin for the two horses. In Bethlehem's bustling market, he traded away his armor for Egyptian robes. Finding young men's clothing was not a problem for a Roman soldier in this small village. The occupation of Palestine had seasoned its citizens to unconscionable acts by many members of the Roman legion. When Decius offered his money to the hawkers in the various stalls in Bethlehem, the response was surprise and then gratitude. The sellers helped him find the best walking sandals for his young friends.

The ornery mule was not nearly as governable as his steeds had been. Home, the dog, helped drive the beast back toward Salome's cove. Decius tore at a loaf of bread and cheese. Maybe the poor beast was hungry. He offered a morsel to the mule, who stepped lively to get his next bite. When the food ran out, Decius ended up pushing and then pulling the mule all the way back to the cove. As he rounded the bend in the late afternoon, he called out, "Ide, come help me kick this mule."

There was no answer.

He signaled for Home to stay near the mule, then ran to where Salome had lain.

They were gone.

The supplies were kicked about. The bread had fallen out of the overturned basket. One wine flagon was emptied and tossed toward the sea. The black puppy scampered from behind the overturned feed sack to greet him. Decius picked up the dog and searched the horizon for movement. When did they leave? Had Herod's troops found Salome and spirited her away? He dropped to his knees in despair. "Lord of Abraham, help me."

The pup licked his face.

Decius called for Home to fetch the mule. He loaded the water skin and the rest of the supplies on the mule, tying the heavy gold-and-bread laden basket to one side of the pile of provisions. His sandal caught in a half-buried braid of Ide's. At least, she had enough time to complete cutting off her hair. Tucking the pup in the breast of his long, belted Egyptian tunic, Decius began his search of the road leading back to Machaerus.

Heat rose off the path in waves of light. One lone traveler approached. A mirage from the heated road produced a shimmering radiance to flow from the man's white, seamless outfit. Decius hailed him. "I am Decius Invictus. I'm searching for my mistress. Have you seen a young girl and her maid on the road from Machaerus?"

The bearded man looked deep into Decius's face, as if deciding whether to give him any information. "I am Jesus the son of Joseph of Heli."

Slipping his Egyptian headgear from his curls, Decius knelt before the man he expected to become king. "I was at Machaerus when Herod ordered your cousin, John the Baptist, slain."

Jesus touched Decius's shoulder. "Do not kneel. You have heard John's words. "My kingdom is not of this world."

Decius stood, feeling his strength renewed after Jesus had merely touched him. He was also surprised that his tongue found words to speak to the holy man. "Your brother Jacob said your mother might offer us a haven."

Jesus nodded as if agreeing with the likelihood of his mother's hospitality. "I'll meet you in Capernaum after 40 days sojourn to the wilderness."

"Lord?" Decius asked, hoping to keep the feeling of peace, which seemed to emanate from Jesus. "I know not how to pray to your Hebrew God."

Jesus bowed his head. "After this manner therefore pray ye: Our Father which art in heaven, Hallowed be Thy name. Thy kingdom come. Thy will be done on earth, as it is in heaven. Give us this day our daily bread. And forgive us our debts, as we forgive our debtors. And lead us not into temptation, but deliver us from evil: For Thine is the kingdom, and the power, and the glory, for ever. Amen."

Jesus stepped off the path and headed west toward the wastelands and the mountain caves of the Essene. Decius felt a strong impulse to follow Jesus anywhere, but he had promised to care for Salome and Ide. Jesus had said he was on a holy mission, a sojourn. Decius continued to stare at Jesus's departure. Did he imagine dust blowing a path before Jesus, or were the beasties of the sand scurrying out of his way?

Home whimpered to get his attention. Decius dropped his hand to the dog's neck. "We need to move quickly. Shall we leave the mule behind?"

Home trotted ahead back toward the mule. Decius shifted the mule's load wondering if he should burden himself with his purchases or leave them, hoping to travel faster. As he took his first hurried steps away, back toward Bethlehem, Home barked. The mule followed, quickening his pace to keep up with his two masters.

Decius determined to keep praying to the Hebrew God, who seemed to be aware of his efforts. But then why was Salome spirited away? Was she safe? He prayed again, "Please Lord of Abraham, provide her safe shelter."

*   *   *

Bethlehem

In the northern outskirts of Bethlehem, Salome cowered behind a roadside boulder as Ide sat begging on the path leading to Jerusalem.

Ide stood when a tall Egyptian came around a distant bend, leading a gray stubborn mule. A dog nipped at the heels of the mule.

"Salome," Ide called. "Stay hidden, but I think Decius is coming."

Salome didn't possess the courage to do more than peek around her hiding place. When the Roman soldiers rode their snorting horses into their camp at the Dead Sea, she thought she might die from fright. She was barely able to walk, let alone run next to Ide to avoid their whips and their horses' hoofs. Because of the bleeding bandages on Salome's legs and arms, the soldiers assumed they were lepers. The men shouted vile things at them, chasing them well away from the paths used by other travelers.

Royal privilege hadn't prepared Salome to live among this beleaguered lower class. How did people survive in constant fear of evil predators? She looked down at her clothing, her maid's rough outer robe, her legs and feet wrapped in bloodied rags. Worst of all, she was hungry.

Ide said they had to be patient, someone would take pity on them.

Salome wasn't sure. She had seen the royal caravans pass by hordes of starving people with their long boney fingers stretched out and even the gaunt faces of children pleading uselessly for food. The elite were deaf to their cries. She knew her people were being taxed to the extreme to pay for all the buildings of her dead grandfather, King Herod, and her stepfather Herod's plans for continued construction of Roman towns proclaiming his loyalty to Tiberius. Her countrymen had to wring their livelihood from the very rocks.

Salome wept for her people and herself. Her stomach hurt and her tongue seemed to be swelling from thirst. She tried to stop crying to conserve any water left in her. She found a smooth pebble and sucked on it to bring saliva to her mouth. She wondered how long it would take to die this way, of starvation, thirst, and degradation.

She closed her eyes, silently repeating David's Psalm to ease her fears. 'The Lord is my shepherd. I shall not want.' But Salome did want. She needed food, water and safe shelter. 'He maketh me to lie down in green pastures. He leadeth me beside the still waters. He restoreth my soul.' Salome did feel an easing of the pain in her stomach. Searching her soul for renewed courage, she only found the desire for its return. 'He leadeth me in paths of righteousness for His name's sake. Yea, though I walk through the valley of death, I shall fear no evil for Thou art with me. Thy rod and Thy staff they comfort me.' Salome rocked back and forth as she pushed her back against the sheltering rock. She felt a little less besieged. 'Thou preparest a table before me, in the presence of those who persecute me. You annointest my head with oil.' Salome thought of the short curls on her head. 'My cup runneth over. Surely goodness and mercy will follow me all the days of my life and I will dwell in the house of the Lord, forever.' The Lord was the only one who could take care of her. She was well aware of that fact.

Salome peeked out at Ide again…and there was golden-headed, blessed Decius offering her water from his supply. She ignored the water and leapt into his arms, holding onto his neck with both hands, kissing his face, his mouth.

Ide pulled at Salome's tunic. "Mistress, control yourself."

*   *   *

Chapter Three

> "…the virgin's name was Mary. And the angel
> came in unto her, and said, Hail, thou that art highly
> favoured, the Lord is with thee: blessed art thou
> among women."
>
> (Is. 7:14; Luke 1:27-28)

Jerusalem

On the road from Bethlehem to Jerusalem, Salome counted the fields where oxen and mules tilled the ground and sowers threw seeds of wheat or barley. She remembered the story of Naomi encouraging Ruth to sleep at the feet of the owner of a barley field. Salome wondered if she would sleep out in the open for the first time in her life. She didn't want to bother Decius to ask, but she imagined it might be fun to count the stars at night. She smelled the wild coriander and dwarf chicory growing in the ditches between the roadside and the farm fields. She was glad to be rid of the bare, dry dessert on the western shore of the Dead Sea. In the green eastern valley, Decius directed them to rest under the shade of one fig and two olive trees.

Ide pointed to a turtledove whose singing was interspersed with the songs of unseen birds in the grove of tall date trees behind them.

Salome remembered the Psalm she'd read when she was under the roof of her father, Philip, 'the righteous flourish like the palm tree, and grow like the cedar in Lebanon.' Would her father know her? She'd grown at least half-a-cubit since she'd left him two years ago. From their

sheltered vantage point on the southern outskirts of the walled city of Jerusalem, Salome watched

pilgrims heading north toward the holy city. They jostled for space with trading caravans headed

south, down to Egypt. The camels bore gum, balm and spices used for anointing oil and fragrant

incenses.

After their respite, Salome held hands with Ide as they skipped behind tall, Egyptian-clad

Decius. Her new sandals flexed with ease and managed to keep the stones and other sharp shards

at bay. She let go of Ide's hand and tapped her beaded cap, which she had placed on her own

short curls.

Ide smiled at her shenanigans.

Proud, Salome was, of many things. One of which was being sly enough to copy Ide's

dressing techniques. She succeeded at her first attempt at pulling on the silk pants and sleeved

vest. Salome hoped her servant didn't realize the freedom and maturity she had gained by not

being clothed by a bevy of maids. Salome's stomach thanked her for its fullness of bread and

cheese. She turned around to check that the water bag Decius had tied to the mule was still fat

with life-sustaining liquid. Maybe she would never want for anything again. Of course, the warm

bed Ide and she shared above the sheepherder's shed last night had helped to alleviate any

immediate fear.

The contrast between Salome's lonely rooms in the Machaerus castle and the comfort

derived by sleeping next to another human made Salome wonder if the rich really knew how to

live. Even the dog, Home, allowed the black puppy to snuggle as close as possible during the

long night. Sharing warmth and touch held a value no one could explain. She hugged the black

puppy she'd named Nether to her cheek. 'Thank you, Lord,' she prayed.

Thinking of King David's dance before the Ark of the Covenant, Salome spun around. No one could recognize her in these boyish clothes, not even her mother. Salome stopped spinning. Herodias was dead to her now, wasn't she? Ide cocked her head to discern the reason for Salome's changed mood. Salome pressed her finger to her lips, so that Ide wouldn't alert Decius to her tears. "Decius," Salome called in a happy sounding tone, "How long before we partake of more food in Jerusalem?" She winked at Ide. "Nether is hungry."

He turned. Home barked at the mule to stop, too. "What? That pinch of a dog can't be hungry so soon after our meal. Maybe he just needs water." Decius poured water from his shoulder flask into Salome's hand.

Salome smiled at her rescuer as she let Nether drink water from her cupped palm.

Decius had kept her at arm's length since she'd kissed him when they were reunited outside of Bethlehem. He'd said her privileged rank required her to act as honorably as if she still lived in Herod's palace. "A princess never takes liberties with her guards," he had said, eyes lowered. Ide had tsk'd her agreement with Decius's advice.

But Salome didn't care. She knew from the first surprising heat in Decius's returned embrace, they shared the same attraction. Besides, no one cared if she was a princess of the realm. Certainly not herself, especially if it meant not being able to touch Decius. Salome looked longingly up into Decius's blue eyes. She reached for his curls, but he stepped away, splashing precious water from the flask he had brought from Machaerus onto the path.

Salome was sure she could wait until Ide either approved or no longer lived with them - to assault Decius again. Her pride wouldn't allow her to entrap a man, would it? If Decius thought she wasn't old enough for him, she could convince him otherwise, couldn't she?

"How many days before we reach Nazareth?" Ide asked, taking advantage of the break to ease her thirst at the water bag as well.

"Maybe ten." Decius frowned in concentration at Home or the mule. "I'll buy more food and find us a place to stay tonight. Be careful to keep yourselves calm as we enter the gates. Salome, keep Nether hidden under your vest. Don't draw any undue attention to us. If the guards detain me with questions, try to stay where I can see you."

"Home will keep us herded together." Ide laughed as she bent down to pet the old dog.

"Does he think we are sheep?" Salome asked. "Tell him, 'the Lord is my Shepherd.'"

Decius's frown hadn't left his face. "Really, don't dance around or say irreverent things as we pass by the guards. You should call me, Master Titus, if the need arises."

"Master, Master," Ide and Salome teased until Decius seemed ready to apply physical threats.

"Sorry," Salome said. "I'm just so happy to be free, Decius. The weather can't be finer. Look how beautiful the Lord's city sits gleaming upon the hills. There's the temple's Dome of the Rock where Abraham went to sacrifice his son, Isaac. Is Rome as beautiful?"

"But you are not yet free from danger, Princess." Decius knelt in front of her. "Help me keep you safe."

"Oh, Decius." Salome refused to cry. She restrained herself from touching his curls, so tempting in their luxurious waves. "Of course, we'll follow your every word. I will never be able to show you how much you mean to me, if I live forever."

Decius stood and bowed before proceeding. Over his shoulder he said, "Someday we will come to terms."

A thrill of excitement passed through Salome. She hid her face from Ide, lest her servant share in her amazement. Decius would someday be hers! Fourteen-year-old Salome kicked a stone away from her path. Someday couldn't come soon enough.

*   *   *

Decius hoped none of the Romans on duty at Jerusalem's gate would recognize him. He had heard Salome mention the Lord again. Was she a willing listener to John-the-Baptist's angry outbursts while he'd been in prison? How did she sort out the prophet's tirades against her mother's marriage to Herod? Could they speak openly in front of Ide, who seemed to adore her mistress?

He allowed himself a smile. The young maidens did look like silly harem boys in their baggy silk pants and beaded caps.

The road was becoming even more congested. Caravans and noisy crowds laden with foodstuffs or pulling along temple animals for sacrifice, jostled with each other through the southern market gate. Decius noticed that the smells of foods, fish, animals, and unwashed sheep farmers wrinkled Salome's delicate nose.

Decius hoped the general mêlée would hide his identity from an older Roman on sentry duty whom he'd recognized. The head centurion, Sextus, was his father's age. Sextus had traveled all the way from Rome with Decius to replenish Pilate's troops. For one homesick moment, Decius was tempted to reach out and ask Sextus for help. But kidnapping Salome, the stepdaughter of Tetrarch Herod, for whatever reason, could get Decius killed.

Salome let out a scream as her puppy escaped from her embrace. Ide quickly grabbed Nether by the scruff of the neck and returned him to her mistress.

Decius tried not to slow his step as he passed Sextus. He wanted to lead the girls into the valley between the temple and the Mount of Olives to circumvent the most crowded sections of Jerusalem. There was enough food for a supper in the gardens surrounding Gethsemane, but he needed more provisions.

Positioning Salome and Ide between the inner wall of the city and the mule, he cautioned them again in quiet tones. "Stay close to me now. I need to buy supplies. Salome, keep your eyes down, so that no one notices their color. Ide stay at her side. Don't let her reach out for tempting articles. Please."

"We're not fools, Decius." Salome pouted, pushing at the mules' side.

"Once we're out of the city, we won't need to be so alert." Decius wondered if he was more afraid for himself or for them. A sense of shame, hiding as an Egyptian, dragging two harem boys to the gods knew where, wounded his Roman pride, but his duty to Salome kept him focused on their immediate safety.

He wasn't only frightened of the Roman officials. Many Hebrews, who might know of Salome's connection to the death of John the Baptist, would want her annihilated. Decius wasn't sure if he'd convinced her to be careful. He didn't want to terrorize the young woman. Even though he wanted to, he couldn't very well carry her through the streets, without someone taking notice.

Ide said the obvious. "Salome knows her peril."

Salome's green eyes tarried too long appraising Decius's resolve. His knees weaken as his desires fought to assert themselves. "Princess," he said, dismissing his baser needs and acknowledging her intelligence.

*   *   *

Salome followed meekly behind Decius as he picked out fruits and vegetables from the plethora of stalls in Jerusalem's packed market street from one end of the old city to the other. Sellers of fresh and salted fish, sandal makers, perfume hawkers, and moneychangers shouted their wares. In the street of spices, the reek of the oil presses, leather shops, and wine booths threatened the air. Down the street of weavers, the tent and sail makers quietly tended to their trades. Salome kept her head lowered, snuggling Nether closer to her chest.

She was fully aware of Ide's nearness behind her every step. Ide whispered warnings, "Don't touch that!" or "They're dirty."

Decius was right to caution her to keep her silence. He often chose the less desirable vegetables when she would have liked more figs and those bright red berries. But she said not a word nor gave any indication that he was doing other than what she considered exactly appropriate. Salome ground her teeth once or twice, when they passed by a perfectly good piece of clothing or the bright red carpet she wouldn't have minded sitting on at their next site for lunch.

When Salome didn't move swiftly enough, Ide tapped her back.

There were jugglers and magic makers, strange animals, and heady perfume stalls. Anyone who wasn't blind or deaf would want to tarry at some of the booths. Even the beggars were sights to behold.

Finally, Decius pulled them through a gate to a quiet walled compound. "I'll seek rooms here," he said. He lifted Salome astride the mule's burdens. "You'll be safe here. Home, stay."

Treated like a dog, was she? Salome's tears slid down her face. She was thirsty and tired of being ignored.

Ide handed her the water gourd to refresh herself. "Mistress, you are very forbearing. We'll be able to let you rest soon."

More tears followed. Dear Ide understood how weary she was. Nether licked some of the falling water from her chin. Salome smiled. "Isn't he a dear, Ide?'

"Except he's a she, Mistress."

Salome laughed. "Oh well, I still love her."

Decius returned, smiling as if he'd heard her laugh. "Plenty of room and they have a wash tub where you may bathe, Mistress."

"Sounds like paradise," Salome said, careful not to hold onto his tunic too long, after he lifted her from the mule. His manly smell fascinated her, but there was plenty of time to explore all the worlds contained in Decius Invictus.

*   *   *

Decius allowed both girls to bathe before he afforded himself the same luxury of cleanliness. Rome's bathing complexes were not duplicated in Palestine. Decius reluctantly redressed in his Egyptian disguise.

The innkeeper provided them a series of sleeping rooms above the stable and bathhouse. He also laid out a dinner of boiled lamb, potatoes and leeks on the rooftop table. The bread and cheese was fresh and the wine refreshing. The girls, dressed as boys, were both in a cheerful mood. They enjoyed watching the older, serious dog. Home tolerate Nether's romping on his back and nibbling at his ears without complaint.

"Ide," Decius began, "Why does your mistress claim the Lord is her shepherd?"

Ide shook her head, claiming the last bit of cheese for the old sheepdog. "Her real father, Philip, taught her to memorize the Psalms."

"No he didn't." Salome tilted her silly cap. "He taught me to read the scrolls."

"Your mother didn't know?" Ide appeared shocked. She explained to Decius. "Women are not allowed to read the holy scrolls." She turned back to Salome. "Do you know God, now that you have read His words?"

Salome cocked her head, then tried to set her cap right. "No more than you, Ide. God is in all of us. He knows our hearts' desires." Salome fluttered her eyelashes at Decius.

Ide failed to notice Salome's flirtation. "But why does God allow evil?"

"Well," Salome reluctantly turned her attention to Ide. "Father read in the first scroll of Torah, Genesis that God allows us to choose to stay with him or to go against his law and leave his presence. Don't you feel better when you know you're doing right?"

"Yes; because I get into less trouble."

Salome reached for Ide's hand. "But you're helping me and you are in danger of Herod's wrath, if they find us."

"No one will recognize either of us." Ide traded caps with Salome, who snatched hers back.

Salome rubbed her hand over her unevenly cut curls. "What did you do with all my hair?"

"I burnt it in the Machaerus fireplace." Ide frowned.

Salome laughed. "It will take 14 years to re-grow it. I'll be 28 years old. Mother's 40. My grandfather, King Herod, died at 40. Did you hear how his stomach burst open with worms while he was still alive?"

Decius nodded. He had heard the story but thought it was only a rumor to show how depraved Herod had been.

"Why are the wicked rich?" Ide persisted.

"I think." Salome hung her head. "Rich means evil. The rich keep more than they need. They throw away what others could use." She straightened and met Decius's eyes. "My father didn't want anyone to deceive me about the word of God." She pushed Ide's cap off her head again.

"Girls," Decius cautioned them to cease their frolicking about. "I mean, boys."

"Ide sings." Salome pushed at her maid's shoulder.

"I don't have my harp," Ide said. "Besides, I'm too tired. May I withdraw, Mistress?"

"Who is she talking to?" Salome asked. "Master Titus, are you hiding a mistress under your robes?" She pushed Ide off her stool. "Take Home with you. You'll need a pillow."

Decius knew he should keep Ide for a chaperone, but he wanted to talk to Salome about her father's beliefs…and hers. "I met the man that John the Baptist called the Christ."

Salome curled Nether into her lap. Her green eyes fixed on Decius, waiting for him to explain.

"When I couldn't find you at the cove, I searched the road back to Machaerus, thinking Herod might have sent soldiers to find you." Decius stacked their empty plates off to one side of the table. "Jesus of Nazareth was all alone on the road, coming toward me. The heat off the road seemed to raise him from the ground. I'm serious. He almost seemed to float as he approached me. The sun made his pale linen robe shine with brilliant whiteness. His eyes held a warmth, an interest in my quest. He agreed with his brother, Jacob, that their mother would provide shelter. But that's not the important thing I wanted to tell you. I felt a sudden peace while I was talking to him. I was so frazzled and without a coherent thought of how to find you two. When he touched my shoulder, all my worries ceased. I told him I didn't know how to pray to the Hebrew God."

Salome held her chin in the palms of her hands with her elbows resting on the table. Decius reached across to set her cap straight. She caught his hand. "We're safe. You're on that side of the table and I'm on this side. We're close enough for all practical purposes." Salome released him. "At least for talking."

Decius smiled at the ornery gleam in her eyes. "Did you listen to John, when he was imprisoned?"

"Mother hated him, so of course I treasured his every word. Tetrarch Herod considered John a true prophet." Salome's face hardened for a minute as she switched subjects. "I don't believe we are supposed to waste time hating anyone. Resentment uses up so much time and it eats into every thought and action."

Decius could see Salome struggling to find something nice to say about her mother. "When I was 10, she told my real father that I was 'as wild as a gazelle.'" She paused, gave up the battle against her ill will and added, "I always hated the high Chaldaean way Mother styled her

hair. Probably just envy, now that I have no hair."

Decius hurried to change the subject less Salome dissolve into tears. "How many Psalms

do you know?"

"Only the one." Salome smiled as she spoke of her father. "I promised to repeat it

morning and evening. When the guards made us leave the cove and called us those terrible

names, I forgot to pray, but when Ide was begging for food, I remembered every word. I was so

frightened. I thought we might die, if you didn't find us soon."

Nether was now on the table, rooting among the dishes for food scraps.

"Jesus taught me a prayer to say," Decius lowered his voice. "Shall I teach it to you?"

Salome smiled. "You like me don't you?"

Decius nodded. "You mean everything to me. You can trust me to bring you to a safe

place where you will be nurtured until you are old enough to know your own mind for adult

decisions."

Salome relaxed in her endearing, winsome way before saying, "I think the Lord has put

me in your path for a reason. I would like to learn the prayer that Jesus taught you."

Chapter Four

"-And Thou Bethlehem, in the land of Juda, art not
the least among the princes of Juda: for out of thee
shall come a Governor, that shall rule my people
Israel."

(Gen. 49:10; Matt 2:6)

Jericho

On the road down from Jerusalem to Jericho, Salome looked back at the walled city

where she could still make out the Tower of Mariamne to the east of the Temple dome. Her

mother, Herodias, might be within hailing distance of the tower. Herod's courtiers would have

returned to the safety of Jerusalem after the beheading of John the Baptist. With no pull of

homesickness, Salome shuddered to think of the evil woman who had given birth to her.

Salome rode the mule while Ide and Decius walked beside her, Ide on her left and Decius

on her right. Ide skipped to keep up with the mule. The home of Ide's parents was in Jericho, but

because of Salome's dangerous flight from Machaerus, Ide fully understood she wouldn't be able

to see them. The loyal serving girl seemed cheered by the familiar scenery or the mere closeness

of her family.

Nether snuggled closer, mirroring Salome's sadness in comparison to Ide's mood. Salome checked on the sheepdog, Home. The hairy black-and-white dog herded them along, switching from one side of the road to the other as if to keep them all together.

The narrow road was crowded with people, who made way for plodding oxen, whose produce-laden carts moved slowly toward Jerusalem and its insatiable demand. The fields of grain along the road were replaced with vineyards as the threesome approached the Jordan River. At one point, the wall lining a vineyard on Ide's side was matched by a high fence on Decius's side of the path. Decius moved ahead of the mule. Ide wasn't as lucky.

The mule shied into the wall, knocking Ide against its rough surface.

Home barked and Salome called out in alarm. Decius stopped and quickly saw the mayhem. He ordered Home to sit between Ide and the mule before he examined the fallen servant.

Salome slipped off the mule. She gently removed her friend's cap. "Did you break the skin?" she asked, fingering Ide's thick, short hair.

Ide pointed to a bump near her ear. "I'm a little dizzy; but I think my hair saved me."

"I wish mine was coming in as quickly," Salome said. "I'm glad you're all right."

Ide accepted a moistened, folded cloth from Decius. "Didn't you tell me a story about a mule talking near Jericho?" Ide asked. "It was after his master beat him for knocking into a wall."

"It was." Salome laughed. "Decius, did you ever hear the story of Balaam's talking ass?"

Decius helped Ide to her feet and continued to watch her carefully as if he expected her to stumble. "Tell us the story," he said. "It's still a long way to Jericho." He lifted Salome up onto the offending mule's back.

Salome wanted to linger in his swift embrace, but Decius was all business. He did pat her hand on the mule's bridle before he turned away. "As I remember it," Salome said, "the mule asked Balaam why he beat her. The mule inquired if she had ever behaved badly in the past. I think the words were, 'Have I been in the habit of doing this to you?' Isn't that funny?"

"Why did Balaam's ass knock into the wall?" Ide clutched her cap in one hand, holding the cool compress to her head with the other.

Salome couldn't remember all the details. "Balaam wasn't supposed to travel in this direction. A Moab king wanted him to curse the newly arrived Israelites from Egypt, but Balaam could only bless them; because, of course, God would not curse us."

Decius chose a large tree whose spreading branches invited them to share the shade with other travelers. They rested in the quiet place and ate their noonday meal. Ide laid her head on docile Home. Salome brought a bit of bread and cheese and then a cup of water to her servant.

Ide's eyes seemed heavy with sleep. She pointed to the shade tree. "Sing to me about the cedars beside the waters."

"You are the singer," Salome protested, but she recited part of Balaam's blessing:

"How beautiful your tents, O Jacob
Your dwelling places, O Israel
Like valleys they spread out
Like gardens beside a river
Like aloes planted by the Lord
Like cedars beside the waters."

Ide interrupted with the lines she'd learned from Salome:

"Like a lion they crouch and lie down,
Like a lioness. Who dares to rouse them?"

Decius became agitated, bending close to Ide and Salome, he whispered, "Those are dangerous poems."

"Why?" Ide and Salome whispered back.

Decius Invictus looked around as if to see if the other travelers had taken any notice. "Never mind," he said. "You two needn't worry yourselves."

But Salome grasped the situation. This blond, bearded man, dressed in Egyptian robes, who seemed besotted with her every move was, after all, a Roman soldier sent to keep the peace in territory ruled by Tiberius. Rousing Jews to rebellion was the opposite of Decius's mission. She made her hand into a claw and snarled at him in jest.

Decius did not laugh.

Home moaned but Ide didn't rouse herself from sleep. Home howled another mournful cry.

Salome shook her maid and called her name softly.

Decius pulled Salome's hands away from her maid. He covered Ide's face with the unfolded cloth she'd held to her bumped head.

Ide wasn't sleeping. Salome looked at Decius to explain how death could have crept into the peaceful grove, snatched her long-time companion from her side, without warning enough to kiss her goodbye, or time to comfort Ide for her travel to the next world.

"I've seen it before," Decius said. "Her injuries were internal."

Salome wanted to protest to someone. "She just spoke to us and remembered the poem." How could life end so quickly, without even a protest of pain from her dear maid?

Home continued to whimper, so Salome let her head drop back and she howled at the injustice of chance, screamed at the black door of death, beat on Decius's chest as he tried to soothe her and crumbled into a useless heap.

*   *   *

Salome insisted Ide's body be taken to the girl's family.

Decius removed one of the golden coils from the breadbasket to bribe three women travelers, who had shared the shaded glen, to return Ide to her parents' home. They promised only to reveal that Ide had fallen against a vineyard wall. Decius fashioned a litter for Home to drag. The oldest women had wrapped Ide's body in a long, white shawl.

Decius comforted Salome. "Ide is not alone. Home will be with her spirit now."

During the remaining trip to Jericho, Salome clung too close for Decius's comfort. She wouldn't ride the mule, gripping his hand, as if he, too, could die without warning.

The fallen walls of Jericho came into view. As they approached, Decius enumerated the ramparts' dimensions recalled from his military studies of the area. "Above that earthen embankment are fifteen cubits of stone, four cubits thick, topped with a mud brick wall, six cubits by two cubits. The ramp to the city was formed by bricks that collapsed after an earthquake."

Salome didn't respond. She walked like a dead person herself: eyes not seeing, her face ashen with grief and fear. She placed one foot in front of the other, but her despair sapped her youthful energy.

Decius couldn't push her away during the following evening. Feeling like an older

brother, he held Salome in his arms until she fell into a fitful sleep. With more of the gold coils

from Salome's fateful dress, he'd paid for the use of an entire house and its cook. The owners

happily took his gold for a week's stay. Decius considered the dwindling number of gold strands;

but Salome's need for privacy as she mourned her maid outweighed his worries.

"Why didn't God take me?" Salome asked in the morning. "I'm the one he should punish,

not Ide!"

Still in their sleeping room, Decius drew the bereaved girl onto his lap, offering his

warmth to ease her pain. "I have no answers for you, Princess." He wiped her teary face before

herding her down to the main room for breakfast. Decius offered her a sip of milk. "Eat now, or

you will make yourself sick with grief."

Nether searched the room for Home. "He misses the sheepdog." Salome pointed to her

sad puppy. "Just like I miss Ide."

"Princess," Decius said, patting her back as if her sobs were burps. "You need to be brave

now. I must leave you here, while I go back to Jerusalem. We can't travel together without a

chaperone."

Salome stopped crying. She pushed him away and got up from the table. With her back to

him, she gazed out the open window. "I don't think I can be alone."

"The cook will take care of you. Her name is Dorcas." Decius walked to where she stood.

He rested his hand on her small-boned shoulder. "I saw a friend of mine from Rome, when we

entered Jerusalem's gate. I need to travel back there quickly. I'll plead with him to find us a

chariot so that we can reach Nazareth as soon as possible. I've paid the cook well. Nether will be

with you."

Decius turned the child-woman he loved toward him. Her stricken face caused him to stop talking. He could smell lingering traces of rose-scented perfumes in her hair. He kissed her soft waves, then placed his huge hand under her dear, pointed chin. He needed to give her enough direction to survive. "If I'm not back by morning, ride the mule north along the Jordan River towards Nazareth. Take Dorcas with you."

Salome slid down the wall into a heap of tears.

Decius called for the cook. "Dorcas."

The heavy-set woman arrived from the kitchen doorway, rubbing her dry hands on a towel. "Come along, child. Your father needs to tend to business. Bring your puppy with you. You can help me chop carrots to add to our soup."

"I need to kiss my father goodbye." Salome jumped into Decius's arms.

Decius turned his back on the cook.

Salome kissed his neck and then stole a sly kiss on his lips before letting him go.

As Decius turned toward the door, a large Roman soldier stepped into the house. "What have we here?" he asked.

*   *   *

Salome grabbed for Decius's arm. He pushed her behind his back as if to shield her from the Roman centurion. "Sextus." Decius said, not letting go of Salome.

"Who are you hiding there?" Sextus stepped closer, reaching out a great meaty paw. His bushy eyebrows rose to a line of frowns, capped by a crown of kinky white hair. "A girl or a boy?"

Decius didn't answer. Instead, he pushed Salome in Dorcas's direction. "Dorcas, weren't you going to serve us food?"

Dorcas took Salome's hand and pulled her into the kitchen, shutting the wooden door behind them. Salome sat down at a small table near the fireplace. Who was the Roman that Decius knew by name, a superior officer?

Dorcas ladled out a large serving of leek soup. She cut an entire loaf of Roman bread, which was an amazing feat since she never stopped looking at Salome. After handing Salome a bowl of soup and still warm slice, Dorcas put the rest of the bread on a tray with two additional bowls of soup.

Salome watched the door swing shut as Dorcas backed her way into the outer room. Then Salome jumped up and reopened the heavy wooden door a crack to listen.

"Jerusalem is awash with gossip," Sextus said.

"Thank you, Dorcas." Decius responded as if afraid of the older soldier's revelation.

Dorcas didn't return to the kitchen. "It's about John the Baptist, I bet." Dorcas contributed.

"You were at Machaerus when Herod ordered his execution?" Sextus asked.

"I was," Decius admitted.

"Then you saw the harlot that danced for him?" Dorcas asked.

Decius didn't answer.

"They say, Herodias's daughter danced." Sextus's voice was low.

As Salome strained to listen, she pushed the door slightly open. Nether whined and scratched at the bottom of the door. Salome picked him up. She placed her stinky soup bowl on the floor for him, before returning with her half-eaten bread to listen to her three elders in the main room. Why had they called her a harlot? Her mother had asked for the execution, not her.

Salome stomach suddenly wasn't hungry, at all. She swallowed painfully. What if Sextus talked

Decius into abandoning her? Would a mob of angry Hebrews stone her? She'd already been

harmed. The evil dress had cut her legs, deeply. One of the scars started to itch as if to prove her

innocence. But, Ide was dead because she tried to help in Salome's escape plan. Poor Decius

could be court-martialed for leaving his post. Salome had witnessed the swift recourse that

captains invoked for deserters.

Salome clutched her throat as if the pain or scream of guilt might escape. She reached out

to her Maker with her skipped morning prayer, whispering, "The Lord is my shepherd." But she

didn't feel the immediate sense of ease which usually accompanied the first words of the Psalm.

What was the prayer Decius had learned from the man John the Baptist called the Christ? Jesus

taught Roman Decius to entreat her Hebrew God. "Our Father."

Yes. A father was better than a shepherd. Tears rolled down Salome's face as she tried to

concentrate on all the words, "Who art in Heaven. Hallowed be Thy Name. Thy kingdom come.

Thy will be done on earth as it is in Heaven." What powerful words. Surely there was only peace

in heaven, no conniving mothers, no vengeful mobs, only justice and understanding.

Hurrying over to Nether, who had emptied the soup bowl, Salome sat on the floor so the

puppy could jump into her lap. She took off her cap and let the dog tug on its beads, as she

recalled the rest of the Lord's prayer. "Give us this day our daily bread."

Salome chewed on the last of her allotment of bread. "And forgive us our debts as we

forgive our debtors." She didn't think she would ever be able to forgive her mother, and who

could forgive her, Salome, the one who danced for John-the-Baptist's head? She picked at the

itching scab on her leg.

Maybe no one in the universe, besides Decius, would ever understand why she had danced for Herod. Perhaps even he didn't realize she only danced for the joy of being alive, as David danced before the Ark. "And lead us not into temptation but deliver us from evil." Salome repeated that plea. "For Thine is the Kingdom and the Power and the Glory for ever and ever. Amen."

Kissing her puppy's nose, Salome felt the peace of God's love expand in her soul. She let go of Nether, reclaimed her cap and pushed open the door to the main room.

Dorcas was asking, "They can't find the dancer?"

Sextus ignored the question. "Someone is providing a refuge from the imperial family." Sextus pointed at Salome. "A girl?"

"I am," Salome said.

"I knew it!" Dorcas slapped her towel against the open kitchen door.

Sextus took note of Dorcas, before asking Decius. "Didn't you think people would notice an Egyptian sporting a blond beard?"

Decius laughed. "It worried me." Then without mentioning Salome's name he introduced the Roman to Salome. "May I present Centurion Sextus Orlando, my father's most faithful friend."

"Then we are not in danger?" Salome asked. She picked up Nether and hugged him.

"That depends on who you are, young lady." Sextus moved closer to examine her.

Decius pulled his Egyptian headgear off. His beard had grown faster than his hair. "I need to take her safely to Nazareth." He walked over and took off Salome's cap.

Salome ran her fingers through her hair. Her strawberry blonde curls were an uneven mass. "Your hair is growing faster than mine."

"Had it cut recently?" Sextus asked.

Dorcas folded her towel into a scarf for Salome, tying the ends behind her neck. "There, now we have our maid."

"And who might you be?" Sextus asked Salome, directly.

Salome looked for guidance from Decius.

Decius shook his head no. "May we extract a promise not to reveal her whereabouts?"

"From the royal family?" Sextus asked, still staring at Salome's green eyes.

Salome blushed. "Please, sir."

Sextus relented and turned his attention to Decius. "You have my word, Decius Invictus."

"Her royal highness, the Princess Salome." Decius bowed to Salome.

Sextus bowed, too.

Dorcas's mouth dropped open. "You're not even full grown. How could the King ask you to dance as a harem girl?"

"My mother ordered the execution." Salome hung her head.

"I witnessed it," Decius said, stepping close and resting his heavy arm on Salome's shoulder. "Herodias made the child drunk with strong wine."

*   *   *

The efficiency which Sextus demonstrated in acquiring more appropriate clothes for a freshly shaven Decius as well as two swift chariots for the trip to Nazareth, made Decius appreciate his father's friend even more. "Will I be punished for leaving Machaerus?" Decius asked, after Salome was occupied in the house helping Dorcas pack food for the trip.

Sextus clapped his shoulder. "Not you. I've covered for you. I told the roster orderly that we were being sent back to Rome by Tiberius."

Decius hung his head. "Won't your superior discover the deception?"

"My superior, Rufus, has been drunk since we arrived in Palestine." Sextus handed Decius another skin of water for the trip. "When he's not entirely crazy and ranting from strong drink, he forgets entire days. He says he depends on me. I'll be lucky if he stays alive, until I can return to Jerusalem. He'll probably be relieved of duty soon."

"I don't know if I can return to duty." Decius checked the harnesses of the team.

Sextus was not without intelligence. "You'll need to survive until Salome is old enough for you to marry. Wait for a few years before you leave the service. We'll find another position for you, away from the palace. Where are you taking Princess Salome?"

"Jesus of Nazareth said his mother lives near the gates in order to give aid to strangers. His brother, Jacob, knew me at Machaerus. He told me their mother is the only one in all of Palestine who might take Salome in."

"Need you keep Salome's identity hidden?" Sextus asked.

"Not from the mother of Jesus," Decius said. He wondered why he knew that was true. "I do know I will not be able to deceive her, even if I wanted to. Jesus is a man of peace. His mother is surely a woman of worth."

"Wealthy then?" Sextus asked.

"I think not," Decius said; although how else could she afford to offer so much aid to strangers?

*   *   *

Journey to Nazareth

Salome counted the days, Decius, Sextus, Dorcas, and Nether traveled together along the Jordan River. Traffic on the roads was never as heavy as the crowds around Jerusalem. The quiet stilled her frazzled nerves, easing her grief over the loss of Ide.

On the first evening, they stopped near a ford across the Jordan River. Rooms in the inns of Salim were not difficult to rent. Sextus generously offered Salome a room with a rooftop terrace for the first night. Nether was growing stronger and Sextus fitted him with a halter which tightened when Salome wanted to control the impish pup.

"I will never be able to repay you for all these kindnesses," Salome told him. "My father, Philip, cannot offer me assistance, lest he feel the wrath of Tiberius."

Sextus bowed. "These are my gifts to your friend, Decius." Sextus pounded his own leather breastplate. "His father charged me with his care."

"Was his father as blond as Decius?" Salome asked.

Sextus laughed. "Indeed, Marcus was every bit as blond as Decius. His mother, Claudia, was the blondest of the three. Her beauty and virtue will never be forgotten in Rome." Sextus's eyes moistened when he spoke their names.

"What's wrong?" Salome asked, touching the old man's arm.

"Surely Decius told you he is an orphan," Sextus said.

Salome cocked her head. "Tell me what happened."

"Princess," Sextus said, "wait until Decius is able to share that knowledge. It's a very painful story."

"I will, Sextus, but please cease calling me Princess." Salome faced the Jordan River view. "It reminds me of a very painful time."

"Shall I call you Salome or some other name?" Sextus asked.

"I probably should change my name," Salome pulled on her curls. "But, I want people to know who I am. Don't I owe others the freedom truth allows them?"

"For a 14-year-old, you are a wise young woman." Sextus bowed his leave, as Decius entered the terrace, with Dorcas on his heels.

Salome smiled at the man she loved. "When we arrive in Nazareth, you'll leave me, won't you?"

"You understand my position," Decius said.

"As well she should, young lady." Dorcas inserted herself into the conversation. "You want him alive, don't you?"

"Safe and secure," Salome said as she accepted his chaste embrace.

*   *   *

On the second day of the trip to Nazareth, Salome tried to reconcile herself to living without Decius at her side. Dorcas rode in Sextus's chariot. Decius's arms wielded the strength necessary to manage the team of four strong horses. She wished the trip would go on forever, so she might never need to miss him. "Will you send messages to me," she asked.

"Better than that," Decius said. "Sextus says I must check on you at least once a month, if my duties permit."

"Are you going to be my husband?" Salome asked.

Decius must have pulled on the reins because the horses changed their pace. He corrected

his grip and tried to face her. "I will never marry anyone but you, Salome. When you are older

and still desire to be my wife, I will know happiness."

"But in the mean-time, the really painful time, we must be separated?" Salome argued

with herself. She looked into her puppy's eyes, trying to keep her feelings in check by

concentrating on the little one's adoration of her.

"I must do what I consider is the honorable thing," Decius said.

"And I," Salome meant her words, but she added, "Although, I wonder if God wants us to

be separated when we love each other so much."

"I will never stop loving you, Salome." Decius's blue eyes widened.

"Nor I you." Salome changed the subject, pointing to the intersection ahead. "Is that the

road to Nazareth?"

Sextus passed them, motioning for them to follow.

*   *   *

Decius likened the valley surrounding the River Jordan to the splendor of the rolling

Italian hills. Green pastures and sprouting fields of grain stretched in every direction. The East

was no longer filled with a wall of mountains. The hills welcomed them as the arms of a mother

might.

The Hebrew people seemed happier this far from the seat of power in Jerusalem. When

they first noticed the two chariots, they didn't react as if they'd just been caught in some thievery.

When they stopped in Bethsaida for the night, the group was greeted amicably rather than as bothersome members of the upper classes. Even Salome relaxed more easily, when Sextus was around.

"She likes you," Decius told Sextus.

"I'm glad," Sextus said. "She is a charmer."

*   *   *

When they reached the hill overlooking Nazareth, Salome asked Decius to stop the chariot. Sextus reined in his team abreast of theirs.

"What a lovely valley," Dorcas spoke for all of them.

Clouds arranged themselves so that an evening glow illuminated the pink-tinted buildings. Built in tiers into the side of one hill, wide streets surrounded and interspersed the terraced town. Golden brambles and purple thistles flowered alongside the lanes, blossoming henna trees formed archways into the small village.

"This must be what heaven looks like," Decius said.

A wagon laden with milled timber approached them from behind. Sextus moved his chariot to the side of the road so that the wagoner could pass. As they neared the town, Salome could hear a pounding. "What's that sound, Decius?"

"I know it." Dorcas answered. "Woodworkers are making furniture."

The house on the approach road just outside the low walls was ringed with gardens of mandrakes and puah, used for dyeing garments.

"Is this Mary's house?" Salome asked Decius.

Decius stopped his horses. "Jacob said the house would be just outside the gate."

Sextus dismounted and approached the entrance of the stone house. Two wings of the house followed the wall. Carved-wooden window boxes held arrays of white lilies and yellow crocus with vines of red roses and purple morning glories nearly touching the ground.

A woman veiled in blue opened the door. She stepped aside to invite them in. "James will help you with your horses. Leave them next to the fence and come in to refresh yourselves."

"We are not staying," Decius said.

"I'm Mary, the widow of Joseph." Mary turned aside to instruct two of her daughters to offer water for the travelers to wash their feet. "Has my son sent you?"

Decius answered, "Jacob encouraged me to bring this young girl to you."

"Yes, he's spoken to me. You're very welcome, Salome," Mary said. "We thought your trip would take longer; but I see you have had the help of your friends."

Salome was awestruck. "Ma'am," she said, bowing to the mother of Jesus. "Decius has taught me your son's prayer to God."

"Jesus has taught us all many things," Mary said. "But come, Decius, bring your friends and break bread with us. Salome, what is your puppy's name?"

Salome felt herself relax as she placed Nether down on the dirt floor. "His name is Nether. We left his friend 'Home' in Jericho, when my maid died." Embarrassing sobs burst from her throat. "Sorry," she said to Decius and Sextus.

Dorcas embraced Salome. "The child is exhausted."

"I have family in Jericho," Mary said, bending down to look directly into Salome's eyes. "We'll send word to your maid's family that we have room for Home, too."

Decius had moved next to Salome. "Jacob convinced us of your welcome, Mary. But now I am assured Salome will be safe and happy under your care."

* * *

Decius found he could not just leave Salome, even if she was under the loving care of Jesus's mother. Decius tried to explain to Sextus, "I cannot abandon Salome. I don't need to live in the same house, but I must remain here. Is there anything you can arrange?"

Sextus agreed some fictitious assignment could be sent from Jerusalem. "Let me find the local officials here, before I promise anything. Dorcas, are you willing to remain in Decius's service?"

"I am," she said. "I'm curious to find out how these two will get together. I mean to see it happens as soon as possible."

Sextus laughed. "Now don't be encouraging the lad. He's already well motivated to that end."

"He is that!" Dorcas said.

Decius joined in the laughter, but he was close to despair. Why did he agree to provide refuge for Salome, away from him? All he really wanted was to be next to her every minute?

The next morning, before the sun had cleared the horizon, Decius found himself standing in the herb garden outside Mary's house. He picked up Nether, who had been busy eating the tops off a row of marigolds lining the path.

Mary opened the door. "Come in Decius. Salome is still sleeping." Mary touched his shoulder. "She cried herself to sleep, so I know she'll be glad to see you."

Decius almost leapt into the house. He wanted to embrace Mary, but instead he sat where she told him to sit, ate what she offered and waited for Salome's appearance.

Mary told him of her plans for Decius to accompany Salome to meet her son, Jesus. "He'll be preaching soon near the Sea of Galilee," Mary said. "Will Dorcas remain with you, too?"

"She will," Decius said. Eventually, he, Dorcas, and Sextus were permanently housed within the walls of Nazareth.

*   *   *

Salome never imagined her stay with Mary would be as carefree as it was. She gladly shared in the household duties. Because Sextus had arranged a job for Decius as the town's governor, Decius came almost every day or at least each evening after his chores administrating the town's affairs were completed. Home was reunited with Nether, who happily jumped around nipping at the bigger dog's paws. Salome wondered if Home still remembered Ide. Salome thought Ide might well be astonished at her new, humble way of life. Mary's female relatives visited often, and Salome shared a room with one of them nearly every night.

Mary's family prayed together each morning and evening. She encouraged Salome to share the Psalm aloud for them all to enjoy. The members of the family varied each day, or so it seemed to Salome. All of Mary's children were grown, but to ensure their mother's safety, one stayed in the home each evening. They brought food on each arrival and cleaned their mother's house, tended her garden and chickens, milked the goats, and ran the household without directions from Mary.

Most of Mary's time was spent teaching children from inside the city's gate various biblical texts from memory. When not otherwise occupied, Mary wove seamless robes for her family and guests. When Salome's robe was finished, Mary helped her dye it a pale green. She also presented Salome with a veil just one shade darker, exactly matching Salome's eyes. Aloe from Mary's garden applied to the scars on Salome's arms and legs helped relieve the itching and discomfort.

One day when the two of them found themselves alone in the house with Nether, Mary asked Salome how she'd come to memorize the one Psalm. "My father taught me to read," Salome said.

Mary hushed her, looking around to see if any family members were within earshot. "You know that is against Hebrew law?"

Nether growled as if suddenly aware of an unseen danger. "I do," Salome said. "But I don't have any opportunity to read now." She bent down to calm Nether's fur. "So, it doesn't matter."

Mary took her by the hand and led her outside and then through the gate into the walled city. "I don't often leave my house."

Mary's statement was immediately proven. Nearly every person they met made a point of speaking to Mary, apparently believing it necessary to explain all the happenings in their families: births, sicknesses, crop failures, betrothals, marriages, deaths. At each bit of new information, Mary nodded, usually touching the face or arm of the speaker before thanking them for their news and moving forward.

"You are mother to them all?" Salome asked, as she adjusted the leash Sextus had made for Nether.

"More like a favorite aunt." Mary laughed.

"You never asked me about Herod." Salome wondered where they were headed.

"You don't need to speak of it, do you?" Mary bent to look directly into Salome's eyes.

"I feel as if you already know what happened."

Mary stroked Salome's wrist. "God knows your heart, Salome; and that's good enough for me."

Salome followed Mary up a slight incline to Nazareth's synagogue. Mary unearthed a large key from a fold in her robe and unlocked a side door. "If you will take over my cleaning duties here, I'll show you why I volunteered for the work."

"I'd be honored." Salome tied Nether to the doorpost. Once inside she appreciated the cooler air in the shuttered building.

Mary locked the door behind them. "No sense being interrupted," Mary explained. Then she opened the doors in the paneled wall behind the flat podium. She lifted out one of the heavily decorated scrolls. "Help me with this, will you?"

Salome pulled the scroll's cover off the sacred Torah. "I don't know all the words."

"My cousin, Elizabeth, was John's mother. She was taught to read by her husband, Zacharias. You remember, John's father wasn't able to speak because he doubted Elizabeth would give birth so late in life."

"I remember some story about his speech being restored." Salome straightened her veil. "When he insisted on naming their son?"

"True." Mary unrolled part of the scroll, searching for the beginning. "Zacharias asked Elizabeth to try to read to him so that he could hear the words aloud. His memory was perfect, so when she stumbled, he would write down the correct pronunciation." Mary dusted the inside of the cabinet where the scroll had been stored with a bit of purple silk cloth.

Salome reached out her hand to examine the silk. "Where does this come from?"

"When my first son, Jesus, was born, visitors from far away brought us many gifts." Mary sat down on a bench closest to the podium. "I need your help, now."

Salome sat next to her, still holding the purple cloth. "I'll be glad to keep the temple clean."

Mary nodded. "If anyone inquires tell them you are cleaning, but I want you to read the sacred words for me." She smiled at Salome's bewilderment. "My eyes have become cloudy and there is still so much I don't know about my son's mission on earth."

Salome stood. "Will the Torah tell us?"

"I'm sure Isaiah's words are meant for my son." Mary said. "Jesus knows the details, but he says I'm not ready to receive all the truth. Do you understand? I want to prepare myself for whatever comes."

"When God's kingdom comes?"

"I'm not sure John meant a kingdom on earth, Salome." Mary bowed her head and folded her hands.

Salome thought she was praying. Instead, she noticed Mary's shoulders started to shake with sobs. "Oh blessed Mother, please don't cry. I won't be able to live if I've saddened you. I'll never leave your side. My mother isn't worthy of my concern. I only want to serve you. Please promise me you will never send me away."

Mary raised her head. She seemed calmed, as if her prayers had restored the wellspring of her soul. "Salome, you will want to marry Decius someday."

"I will," Salome admitted. "But does that mean I would need to leave you?"

Mary got to her feet and embraced her. "I promise, where ever I go, you may follow, if you choose. Will you, then, search the Scriptures?"

"I will," Salome promised, realizing she had secured a permanent home for herself.

"Thank you."

Chapter Five

"The people which sat in darkness saw great light;
and to them which sat in the region and shadow of
death light is sprung up."

(Is 9:1, 2; Matt 4:16)

Nazareth, Late Nisan (March)

One night at dinner, Decius described to those assembled how he had met Jesus on the

road from Machaerus. Sextus voiced his curiosity to see and hear the prophet that John the

Baptist had anointed. Decius surmised that Salome was somehow involved in Mary's conviction

that Jesus had returned from his spiritual quest and would soon preach in Nazareth's synagogue.

Decius had raised his eyebrows after Mary's remark, wondering what the basis of their

conjecture was.

As if in explanation, Salome told him, "I have taken over Mary's caretaking duties in the

synagogue."

Decius wondered what that included. When he met Salome as she returned from the

synagogue toward Mary's house in the evening, she hadn't been at all interested in him. Usually

Salome would grab his arm and kiss his face, if the street wasn't too crowded; instead, Salome

almost ran past him in her rush to speak to Mary.

Home had seemed upset as he circled Decius before deciding to follow Salome and Nether. He looked back once at Decius with his nose lowered in disapproval, as if to encourage Decius to follow them with due speed.

"I've found something for Mary," Salome explained; but she wasn't carrying anything.

Decius thought she might have had an inspiration from her Hebrew God. He couldn't be sure. The two women were careful not to allow him close enough to hear when they were gossiping as they had laid out the food. He noted their excitement all through the evening meal; but they failed to enlighten him as to the cause.

Finally, he decided he could no longer tolerate his frustration. After Dorcas and Sextus returned to their rooms over Nazareth's sentry station, Salome walked outside with the dogs and him for their evening's goodbye embrace. So, Decius asked her, "Do you keep secrets from the man you are going to marry, someday?"

"Oh!" Salome seemed surprised by the question. "Wait here. I must ask Mary if I have her permission to tell you." She ran back into the house.

Home barked at her sudden departure, but laid down at Decius's feet. Nether promptly jumped on the older dog's back, trying to wrestle. Decius sat down on the stone bench in the herb garden. He didn't wait long before Salome returned.

Her face was flushed when she sat next to him. "Mary says, of course, you must know. I'm reading the Torah and the scrolls of the Prophets. Mary's eyesight is getting a bit cloudy with age. You know it is against our laws, but husband and wives can have no secrets, ever."

Decius laughed with relief. "I'm so proud of you, Salome." He picked up Nether in order to hug something. "You will make a virtuous and educated mate, a woman any man would be proud to marry. What did you find today? You both seemed so excited?"

Salome laughed and brushed the air, as if nothing important had occurred. "Mary already knew the passage from Genesis, 'And Thou Bethlehem in the Land of Juda, art not the least among the princes of Juda: for out of thee shall come a governor, that shall rule my people Israel.'"

He couldn't help himself. He carefully released Nether, then enclosed Salome in his arms, kissing her innocently on the lips. "Salome, do you remember when I hushed you and Ide? She wanted you to recite Balaam's prayer. It contained worrisome ideas, too."

"The word 'governor,' is a problem." Salome hung her head. "For a member of the occupation forces to hear?"

"John the Baptist taught your Savior's reign would be in the world to come." Decius had released his beloved, but they remained close enough to feel each other's warmth and affection.

Salome nodded, then laid her head on Decius's shoulder. She whispered, "I don't know if you want to bring Sextus, but Jesus might be speaking tomorrow morning at the synagogue."

"We'll be there." Before he took his leave, Decius enjoyed one more kiss from his willing partner.

*   *   *

Salome and Mary joined the other women in their separated portion of the temple. The crowd of whispering females parted to allow Salome and Mary a place near the openings in the latticed screen. Salome thought she noticed Mary's hands shaking, but the blessed woman folded them under her blue robe, so that Salome couldn't really be sure she'd witnessed the mother of Jesus being nervous for his first sermon.

Jesus was taller than the rest of the congregants, almost as large as a Roman. Salome spotted Decius and Sextus. Even though they wore modest robes over their military clothing, their height gave them away.

After a call to prayer, the oldest rabbi invited their wandering neighbor to speak.

Jesus removed the scroll containing the words of Israel's prophets. He didn't hurry the process of removing its covering and laying it gently on the podium. Jesus added to the drama by lengthening the time needed to find the passage He wanted. Finally, He raised His head and smiled at the attention of His audience, nodding in the direction of Mary. His Hebrew chant was deep and sonorous, as if the desert sun had parched His throat. "Isaiah says at the beginning of the 61st section, 'The Spirit of the Lord is upon me, because he hath anointed me to preach the gospel to the poor; he hath sent me to heal the brokenhearted, to preach deliverance to captives and recovery of sight to the blind, to set at liberty them that are bruised, to preach the acceptable year of the Lord.'" Jesus surveyed his rapt listeners before adding, "This day is this scripture fulfilled in your ears."

A hush ensued. Mary turned away, smiling her pleasure. Salome followed her out of the synagogue into the street. The dogs romped around them as they proceeded down the hill toward their home outside the city's gate. "It has begun," Mary said.

Salome wished they had stayed a while longer. "Do the others believe Jesus?"

"That question will need a private answer," Mary said. "Now we best lay out the welcoming feast for my wayfaring son."

*   *   *

Sea of Galilee

For their walking tour to the Sea of Galilee, Decius and Sextus again wore the robes Mary provided to cover their military-issued garments.

Salome rushed out the door to follow them. Nether was jumping around her excited by their preparations for the trip. "Decius, wait. Mary wanted me to bring more food." She handed Sextus and Decius each a leather satchel of provisions. She carried the water skin. "Yours are heavier," she explained. "We need to return by way of Cana, where Mary's relatives are celebrating a wedding. She says we have plenty of time."

They headed due east to the southern tip of the Sea of Galilee. Herod had improved the road from Nazareth to the Jewish graveyard, before desecrating the site with the Roman town he named for Tiberius. The early morning sun glistened on the dew-sprinkled grasses. Salome saw two white cabbage butterflies dance in the sun's warming beams. She pointed to them, but Decius was in a serious discussion with Sextus. Nether spied the butterflies and tried to jump as high as the insects. They darted around his head as if to tease him. Home was in his favorite element, happily herding the group towards the sea.

"I'll need to report to Pilate," Sextus was saying, "if this prophet is preaching rebellion."

Decius argued with his elder, "Wait until you speak with Him. Did you think He appeared as the type of man to encourage violence? When I remember our brief encounter, my mind almost hums with a peaceful realization of harmony with the entire universe. I can't put my excitement into words."

"You always were a poet. The crowds attending this man are the same people who chased John the Baptist. They could pose a threat to Herod." Sextus laughed, as if at his own fears, and gestured to Salome. "Does Decius recite his poetry to you? Is that what drew you together?"

Salome shook her head. "Decius, recite one of your poems."

Sextus laughed, again. "He will orate all the way to the sea now."

Decius blushed, which Salome didn't hold against him. His first poem was rather short. The careful spacing of his words kept time with their steps on the paved road.

"Unrenowned," Decius began. "Earlier than some now, my staccato songs still bray as loud as the public's scowl of rejection. My soul neverminds because he's keeping company, gives affection back to His universe of creation."

Sextus patted Salome's shoulder. "Don't try to understand them. It's hopeless."

Salome tilted her chin, feeling justifiable pride in Decius. "The poem is perfectly simple: Decius's fame as a poet hasn't been fully realized, but he's not discouraged, because he's thankful the Lord has given him such a gift."

"You two are meant for each other." Sextus nodded as Decius gave Salome a quick hug.

"Hebrews possess a natural ability," Decius said, "Their language sways up and down the musical scale, making each word into individual songs."

Salome gladdened her heart. This man of hers was not a snob like other Romans she knew, who refused to speak anything but Greek to each other when they were in public. They acted as if the slang of their native language was beneath them, however, Salome conceded the sacred Hebrew was a more sonorous language than the whiney Latin or unpronounceable Greek.

They stopped once for a hasty meal then rushed on toward the sea to arrive in time to catch an evening vessel for their trip north to Bethsaida, where Jesus told his mother he was headed. However, Salome noticed Sextus was becoming exceedingly tired. He stopped often with the excuse of petting or giving water to Home. "Perhaps we could catch a ship in the morning?" Salome motioned with her head for Decius to become aware of Sextus's weariness.

Sextus interpreted Salome's gesture, too. "I'm a Roman," he said. "We march until we drop, don't we, Decius."

Home barked as if he agreed with the loud statement.

"Should we stop, Sir?" Decius asked.

"Don't embarrass me, you two." Sextus laughed. "Wait until you're my age and younger people want you to slow down, then you'll know how I feel."

Salome touched Sextus's hand. "We'll go on. I forgot how far Caesar marched to conquer nations."

"Please," Sextus said. "I am too tired to defend my Caesar."

"I should hope so," Decius said.

Salome noticed Sextus's frown did not quickly leave his brow. "It is good that we are friends and can trust each other," she said to emphasize the importance of being able to speak freely.

"Never fear, Salome," Sextus said. "Decius's father entrusted his son to my care. No one will bring harm to him or his, not even me."

Salome noticed Home licked Sextus's hand, as if he had understood every loyal word.

                                   *   *   *

After boarding, Decius hoped the rocking ship would let him sleep as peacefully as the dogs, and Salome and Sextus, but his mind raced with the possibility of hearing Jesus speak again. His recitation from Isaiah in Nazareth's synagogue convinced Decius this prophet was Palestine's Messiah. Would Jesus now gather warriors to overthrow the yoke of Rome? If that happened, where would Salome and he stand? Would she turn against him, against his love for her? Would he end up living alone in the world again?

Decius watched the sky lighten as dawn approached. He remembered how threatening the day's arrival seemed to him, when he first spirited Salome away from Machaerus. No hazards could stop him now; instead he wanted to pull the sun up with his bare hands.

While he was standing at the railing of the ship, one of the older sailors joined him. "Always a refreshing sight," he said.

Decius smiled at the man. "This day is not like any other day."

The fisherman closely assessed Decius, measuring his height, sounding his depth. "That saying is part of an evening prayer at Passover. Only the word 'day' is 'night'. *Ma nishtanaw haliola hazeh shebicol haliola.*"

Decius caught a sudden sob in his throat at the beautiful sounds of the words. "Thank you," he said, trying not to let his unexpected emotion overwhelm him.

*   *   *

Bethsaida

When they reached the northern shore of the Sea of Galilee, on the western side of the Jordan River's entrance, Salome could see Bethsaida perched on top of a steep embankment. The path from the dock up to the city crossed a line of ancient walls, clearly visible to the left. The large gate of the city led to a paved area separating the outer gate from the inner gate. The inner gate was flanked by standing stone slabs, taller than Decius and Sextus, even if one stood on the shoulders of the other.

On the north side of this courtyard, three steps led up to a small platform with a shallow stone basin. Chambers on each side, just within the gate were in the form of an 'E' facing a mirror image. Fishmongers and fishermen and their workers filled these areas with their hauls of the day. Ropes and pulleys were erected to pull the netted fish up from the boats to the level of the courtyard market. Trammel nets filled with the catch of the day were let down from the shoulders of weary men.

Salome was glad the activity helped them to blend in with the crowds entering the inner gate. Nether's strong leash helped Salome control the dog's curiosity about each new smell. Home was not happy with the crowds. He often barked if someone came too close. Salome knew Decius and Sextus lost any chance of disguise solely on the fact of their height.

In the northeast corner of the town, a large wooden tower was erected. Salome heard Decius ask Sextus the reason for what appeared to be an observation tower. "I've seen these in fishing villages around the Mediterranean," Sextus said. "They're racks for preserving fish for transport. The air dries the fish."

The streets in the middle of the town were paved with a mixture of sand and black volcanic dust. The first building they passed was built around two sides of a courtyard opening to the street. Large stone jars of wine vied with each other for space in the storehouse of the grape grower.

The next house was constructed around three sides of a paved courtyard where Salome was surprised to hear Greek being spoken by two of her countrymen. She boldly called to them in Greek, asking where they traveled from.

"I am Andrew, the son of Jona," the older of the two men answered in Hebrew. "This is Philip. Welcome to the home of fishermen. My brother, Simon, and I were born here along with Philip. James and John the sons of Zebedee work with us, too. How may we help you?"

Decius answered for them, "We seek Jesus of Nazareth."

The fishermen shared a look of understanding. Philip spoke, "Did you fail to notice the crowd on the shore listening to his words? We were just going down to join them. Jesus has called Andrew, Simon, whom he calls Peter, and me to become his apostles and to follow him"

The road Philip and Andrew chose to return to the seashore was lined with fig trees. Under one of the trees, a man called out to Philip. Andrew whispered to Decius, "The man's a publican, a tax collector."

Salome watched Sextus's reaction to the derision implied by Andrew's tone. She could tell Decius and Sextus were silently weighing their options as Romans in disguise. Nether and Home reacted to the growing tension by growling at each other.

Philip saved the men from making any negative comments. He called out, "Nathaniel, we have found him of whom Moses in the law and the prophets wrote, Jesus of Nazareth, the son of Joseph."

Nathaniel said, "Can any good thing come out of Nazareth?"

Philip said, "Come and see."

As the small group approached the growing crowd of listeners, Jesus saw Nathaniel coming toward Him and said, "Behold an Israelite indeed, in which is no guile!"

Nathaniel said to Him, "Whence knowest thou me?"

Jesus answered, "Before that Philip called thee, when thou wast under the fig tree, I saw thee."

Nathaniel said, "Rabbi, thou art the Son of God; thou art the King of Israel."

Jesus said, "Because I said unto thee, I saw thee under the fig tree, believest thou? Thou shalt see greater things than these. Verily, verily, I say unto you, hereafter he shall see heaven open and the angels of God ascending and descending upon the Son of man."

Salome and Sextus tried to catch Decius as he fell to his knees. Jesus raised a hand in their direction, as if in recognition of the spiritual awakening in one Roman's soul.

*   *   *

After they secured housing arrangements in a pleasant inn facing the sea, Decius tried to describe what had happened. "My soul has thirsted for an unnamable relief since I can remember. My place in Palestine creates so many vying perspectives of everything." Decius paced the dining room, going first to Sextus's place at the table and then to Salome's, trying to explain. Home eyed him from his position before the fire, but Nether tagged behind his every step. "I thought I might be torn apart inside my skin," Decius said, then added as reassurance, "I love you, Salome."

Decius walked out onto the small balcony. The gathering evening held the promise of a beautiful new day. The cacophony of bird song nearly deafened his new awareness. Nothing clouded his mind. He thought his sight had improved, too. He could see all the way to the seashore, where fishermen were laying out their intricate fishnets, the smell of mountain air from heaven's gates refreshed his lungs, the taste of honey sweetened his breath. He picked up Nether for a quick embrace and then set the dog down. "Now I see how everything fits together. My heart or soul seems expanded. The very light of Rome, the night of Israel, the day of a new world has descended on me. I am no longer Decius Invictus, but a new being." From the balcony, he turned toward them and spread out his arms to enclose them. "Did you not feel the power of His love?"

Sextus lowered his head to his chest before answering, "I understand why you need to believe. I've tried to provide the affection your parents would have lavished on you, but I know I was less than the task required."

Salome flashed her green eyes at him. They danced in a pool of tears. "Are you still in need of a bride?"

Decius was struck mute in astonishment. When he had sufficiently recovered, he said in a quiet voice, "I know you both love me, but this is bigger than any of us. There is no one I cannot love now. I think God wants us to love each other with the strength of the love I now feel from Him. There is nothing in the world that I want but to be close to the Lord."

Sextus stood up and blocked the door. "You are not going to become one of His followers."

Home groaned when he rose to join Sextus at the door.

Decius laughed. "No, Sextus. My commitment to Salome and to your kind offices has not changed. My soul has changed. It magnifies the Lord."

Salome began to weep. "Mary said Jesus would separate believers, sons from mothers, wives from husbands, parents from their children."

Nether tugged at the hem of her tunic, as if to cheer her.

Decius knelt in front of Salome, taking her delicate hands away from her sweet face. He kissed her forehead, her lips, embraced her. "Salome, look into my heart. Do you see I've changed in my love of you?"

Salome lifted her wet eyelashes and looked deep into his eyes. "I only see the man I promised to marry."

Sextus sat back down. "We're all right then. We have not lost our place in the world."

Decius smiled. They had not been able to understand the great blessing he had received. 'Please, Lord,' he prayed, 'enter their humble hearts, as You have mine.'

*   *   *

When Salome opened the door of their rented rooms to let Nether out for the morning, she recognized Nathaniel from his rich, purple robes. "Blessings on your day," she said. "My men folk are still abed."

"The Lord has asked me to remind you, Salome." Nathaniel touched the doorframe's Jewish icon as he entered. "Mary needs your help for the wedding feast in Cana."

Salome tilted her head, wondering how Nathaniel was involved in the wedding.

"Cana is my home town," Nathaniel said in reply to her implied question. "The wedding feast is being held at my family's estate. Jesus wants us to journey together. I know the easiest route and inns that will accommodate us. I'll be driving a cart with six jars of wine for the wedding. Will you be traveling on foot with the rest of Jesus's disciples?"

"I'm not sure. Let me offer you bread and cheese." Salome pointed to the long table behind her. A basket of fruit invited guests to partake. "I'll wake Decius and Sextus." Salome turned to go.

But, Nathaniel called after her, "Jesus told me that Decius is a believer like me."

"I believe in the Lord," Salome said. "Why do you only mention Decius?"

"You believe in the father of us all." Nathaniel sat down on the long bench at the wooden table. Nether chose to attack Nathaniel's trailing robe. Salome called his name but he wasn't a very obedient dog. Nathaniel let the puppy play tug-of-war with him for a moment, before tucking the robe's ends under his knees. He cut himself a piece of cheese, throwing a nibble to Nether. Then he said, "Decius and I believe Jesus is with us here on earth to deliver the world from all our sins."

Salome didn't understand, so she nodded and went to fetch Decius and Sextus.

*   *   *

Cana (Kafr)

Decius's face had frozen into a permanent smile. He rubbed his cheeks which ached from his overt happiness. As far as he was concerned, their trip from Bethsaida to Cana could not have been easier if they had tread on the streets of paradise. The sky refused to rain, the roadbed was soft, and the first flowers and birds of spring outdid themselves to serenade and refresh the troupe. Home and Nether filled out their ranks with Nether's high jinks and Home's courteous concentration on keeping his growing herd together. Nathaniel's trading acquaintances had housed and fed them on the one evening they spent on the road.

Jesus followers did include the crowds who had sought out John the Baptist. Jesus named several men his apostles, along with Simon, whom Jesus called Peter, Andrew and Philip also left their boats in Bethsaida to follow Jesus's call as did the rather short sons of Zebedee, John and James, marching on either side of Jesus in front of Nathaniel's large cart and team of oxen.

Matthew, another apostle and a rich publican like Nathaniel, shared the duties of driving the team of oxen. Jude and Janus, the son of Alphaeous and Lebbaeus, whose surname was

Thaddaeus, were also considered apostles of Jesus. This Janus was as tall as Sextus. The two of them kept Salome and Nether striding safely between them.

Decius heard Salome ask Janus how far Cana was from Mary's home in Nazareth. "Jesus's mother probably stayed the night in Cana," Janus answered. "The distance is only an afternoon's walk from Mary's home."

Now on the last leg of the trip to the wedding feast, Decius enjoyed arguing with Thomas, who doubted many Jews would ever accept Jesus as their Messiah. Decius thought he knew better. "Once they experience the redemption we share, their defenses will disappear."

Thomas pointed to Sextus and Salome. "And yet your friends hesitate."

"The Lord will open their hearts, when they're ready." Decius prayed unceasingly for that miracle to happen as soon as possible. His love for both of them had not changed, but a valley of misunderstandings was widening between them, separating their hearts from his.

Judas Iscariot, who counted the money given to the Messiah, brought up the rear of the group with Simon the Canaanite and the very rotund Bartholomew acting as his guards. Home trailed behind them.

The poor and sick who lived in squalor on the periphery of the villages they passed posed no threat to them. Jesus approached each group they encountered, blessing the diseased after assuring them their sins were forgiven. Decius watched the shunned people, who believed illness was God's punishment, quickly recover their dignity, if not their health. Jesus's affirmation of their right to be on God's good earth was a powerful stimulant for healing.

*   *   *

When the caravan arrived at Nathaniel's home in Cana, Salome noticed empty,

earthenware vessels, once filled with wine for the feast, were cast alongside the outer wall. The

wedding celebration had already begun. Nathaniel's supply of stone jars, holding three or four

firkins of wine each would be welcomed.

Mary greeted them at the entrance hall of the large complex. Younger women carrying

towels and shallow water basins offered to wash the travelers' feet. Mary told Jesus, "There is no

wine."

Jesus answered and said, "Woman, what have I to do with thee? Mine hour is not yet

come."

Salome watched as Mary directed the women servants. "Whatsoever he saith unto you, do

it."

And there were set there six waterpots of stone, after the manner of the purifying of the

Jews, containing two or three firkins apiece. Jesus saith unto them, "Fill the waterpots with

water." The young servant girls rushed about and filled them up to the brim. At the same time

Nathaniel, Matthew, Janus, and Sextus brought in the six stone jars of wine from Bethsaida,

pushing the filled water jars to the side. Jesus saith unto the servants, "Draw out now, and bear

unto the governor of the feast."

James and John, the sons of Zebedee, Decius and the rest of the apostles were busy

toasting the bridegroom inside with the new wine. When the ruler of the feast had tasted the

wine, and knew not whence it was: (but the servants thought the water had been changed into

wine); the governor of the feast called the bridegroom, and saith unto him, "Every man at the beginning doth set forth good wine; and when men have well drunk, then that which is worse; but thou has kept the good wine until now."

Salome wondered if she should correct the servants, who were excitingly whispering to John and Decius. She busied herself with pouring water into a basin to refresh the dogs. Belief continued to elude her; even though, she thought this small misunderstanding was harmless, it was a stumbling block for her trust in Jesus's new influence over Decius.

Sextus nodded in Decius's direction, clearly understanding her dilemma. "We should join the wedding party," he said as he took her arm.

Salome motioned for Home to stay outside. Nether lay down beside him.

Chapter Six

"My house shall be called the house of prayer; but
ye have made it a den of thieves."

(Is 56:7; Mark 11:15)

Capernaum

After listening to Jesus preach in the small, limestone synagogue at Capernaum, Sextus

asked Decius to return with him to Nazareth. Dorcas had sent word that she was not well.

Decius felt torn between wanting to stay near the Savior and his obligations to Sextus and

Dorcas. Salome and Mary planned to return home too, before making the yearly trip to Jerusalem

for Passover. Finally, Sextus agreed the rest of them should stay one more day with the apostles

and Jesus before bringing the travelers back to Mary's house in Nazareth. Provisions needed to

be readied for the long Passover trip to Jerusalem.

Sextus commandeered a swift chariot to return to their servants' side in Nazareth. Salome

asked him to take Home and Nether with him, so that the dogs wouldn't be worried by the

growing crowds surrounding Jesus in Capernaum. Nearly every one of the thousand citizens of

Capernaum and people from all over Galilee seemed intent on personally speaking with Jesus.

When Decius reached Peter's stone compound with the apostles, they found Peter's

mother-in-law in bed with a high fever. Jesus took the older woman's hand and the fever immediately left her. She sat up in her bed, then rose and began to prepare them an evening meal in one of the separated sheds.

The central building of drystone basalt housed a dining room plastered inside with a whitewash of limestone. The twelve apostles arranged themselves on benches attached to a long, wooden table. Unlike the paved courtyard, the floor of the room was tiled with black basalt cobblestones. Decius supposed Salome had followed him into the house, but when he searched for her to sit with him for the meal, he couldn't find her. When he called her name, she answered from just outside the door. He could see Mary and her son, Jacob, were close to the entryway, too.

When Decius told Jesus that his mother and brethren remained outside, Jesus said, "Who is my mother? And who are my brethren?" And he stretched forth his hand toward his apostles at the table and said, "Behold my mother and my brethren! For whosoever shall do the will of my Father which is in heaven, the same is my brother and sister and mother."

Because of the press inside the room, Decius couldn't return to Salome and Mary. He hoped they had heard Jesus explain why he didn't make space available for them at the table. He wished Sextus had stayed to help him maintain some kind of order in the developing mob of sick and troubled people descending on Peter's compound.

After the sunset, people began pulling off the thatched roof of the dining room, in order to gain access to Jesus's preachings. Through the freshly opened roof, four men lowered a bed with a young man lying on it shaking with palsy.

When Jesus saw their faith, he said unto the boy, "Son, thy sins are forgiven thee."

Now religious leaders had been admitted to the house because of the crowds' respect and fear of them. They were standing along the wall with Decius, who overheard them say to each other, "Why doth this man thus speak blasphemies? Who can forgive sins but God only?"

Jesus answered them, as if they had spoken directly to him. "Why reason ye these things in your hearts? Whether it is easier to say to the sick of palsy, Thy sins be forgiven thee: or to say, Arise and take up they bed and walk. But that ye may know that the Son of man hath power on earth to forgive sins," He said to the boy, "I say unto thee, arise and take up thy bed and go thy way into thine house."

The amazed crowd at the door parted, singing praises to God. And the boy walked out to his home, a restored man.

After the crowd dispersed, Decius wandered between the houses grouped around an irregular, deserted courtyard, overworking his mind to take in the new terrain of his soul. The darkened sky revealed a full moon dancing among heaven's stars. With his head in the clouds, Decius nearly stumbled over Judas Iscariot, who crouched on the ground with his back to Decius.

Decius was about to call out, when he noticed the glint and sound of coins. Judas was burying his collection of donations for Jesus's ministry under one of the flagstones in the courtyard, behind Peter's dining room. Decius's first thought Sextus would know what to do, or who to tell. As Decius backed away, he realized he didn't trust this one apostle of the twelve called by his Savior.

In the dark courtyard, Jesus touched Decius's shoulder and motioned for him to follow. As they walked along the broad streets of Capernaum, Jesus stopped before a building, where man-made pools lined two sides of the walls. Fish broke the surface of one of the keeping ponds, breaking the reflection of the moon's glow.

Jesus spoke in a hushed tone. "The Son of man shall be betrayed into the hands of men; and they shall kill him and the third day he shall be raised again."

Not understanding the full meaning of the Savior's words, Decius was comforted to know that Judas's actions had not gone unnoticed by Jesus. "What would you have me do, Lord?"

Jesus raised his hand as if overcome with emotion. "God's will be done."

Decius didn't walk back with Jesus to Peter's house, instead he continued alone around the streets of Capernaum, wondering at the Lord's words and actions, unable to fathom the implications to Palestine's future under Roman rule, or the tragic fate Jesus, of His betrayal and death.

*   *   *

Earlier when the crowd started pulling off the roof of Peter's dining room, Jacob insisted they leave to find Salome and his mother, Mary, a place to stay the night. Salome pleaded with him to send a messenger back to Peter's house, so Decius would know where to find them on the outskirts of Capernaum.

Her tall Roman poet arrived early the next morning; his eyes were glazed with more than fatigue. Decius insisted on relating every word spoken by Jesus as well as every healing, then he muttered, "The Jewish religious leaders are not encouraging Him to continue his ministry."

Mary finally demanded Decius cease talking. "At least lie down for an hour before we all return to Nazareth. Jesus will ruin His health if He keeps letting these people drain His energy."

On the way out of Capernaum when Jesus and the apostles joined them, Salome saw Sextus stop his chariot in front of Jesus's path.

Sextus beseeched Jesus, "Lord, my servant, Dorcas, is at home sick of the seizures and is grievously tormented."

Jesus said, "I will come and heal your servant."

Sextus answered, "Lord, I am not worthy that thou shouldest come under my roof: but speak the word only, and my servant shall be healed. For I am a man under authority, having soldiers under me: and I say to a man, Go, and he goeth, and to another, Come, and he cometh and to my servant, Dorcas, Do this and she doeth it."

And when Jesus heard it, he marveled and said to them that followed, "Verily, I say unto you, I have not found so great a faith no, not in Israel. And I say unto you. That many shall come from the east and west, and shall sit down with Abraham and Isaac and Jacob in the kingdom of heaven, but the children of the kingdom shall be cast out into outer darkness. There will be weeping and gnashing of teeth." And Jesus said unto Sextus, the centurion, "Go thy way; and as thou has believed, so be it done unto thee."

Sextus turned his chariot around and drove his team toward Nazareth.

*   *   *

Nazareth

When Salome, Decius and the rest of the travelers reached Mary's house outside Nazareth's gate, Sextus and Dorcas were waiting to greet them. Dorcas was healed the selfsame hour that Jesus spoke. Sextus and Decius embraced for a long time, kissing each other's cheeks like Hebrews. Abandoned to seek her own solace, Salome joined Dorcas helping with Mary's food preparations for the long trek to Jerusalem.

But Mary had taken note of her mood. "They're not excluding you, Salome. They're deepening each other's understanding of the Lord's miracles in their lives." Mary reached under Salome's veil to tug at her hair. "I have a friend of Jesus's with the same color hair as yours. I want you to meet. Her name is Mary, like mine; but we call her Magdalen."

Dorcas sucked in her breath for some reason, but Salome didn't ask why.

*   *   *

Jerusalem

Sextus pulled Decius aside, after Mary introduced them to Magdalen. "I have carnal knowledge of this woman." Decius waited to hear more, but Sextus scratched his head, turning the subject to a more pressing matter. "If the number of people Jesus gathered in Peter's house decide to descend on Jerusalem for their religious holiday, I should put my troops on alert."

"You know Jesus is not interested in an earthly kingdom." Decius was sure Sextus had experienced a similar awakening in his soul.

Sextus nodded. "But those around Him might have other ideas and start something not stopped by prayer alone."

Decius decided to confide in Sextus. "I already saw the apostle, Judas Iscariot, bury a huge sum of money under a flagstone behind Peter's house."

"How much money?"

"My curiosity got the best of me and I went back to count." Decius decided not to share Jesus's prediction of betrayal and death. "There are 282 dinars buried. I don't know for what purpose."

"I'm going ahead," Sextus said. "I'll give orders to only keep the peace."

Decius wanted to mount a chariot and flee from his worries; but his commitment to Salome kept him close. After the wedding in Cana, he hoped Salome might think about their wedding, but she seemed preoccupied with the subject of wine jars and he couldn't keep her attention long enough to propose.

On the road down to Jerusalem, Decius marveled at the religious zeal of the Hebrews. They herded their choicest livestock of oxen and sheep to be sacrificed for their redemption on the altar of Jerusalem. Rome's citizens were a superstitious lot, but they lacked genuine, overt devotion to any of their gods.

He noticed his original feelings of rapture had been replaced with fear for the safety of Jesus and the rest of their caravan. Decius prayed for their safe journey.

*   *   *

Salome's deepest being registered the change in Decius. She came up behind him jumping up to tap his shoulder as a cheerful tease.

Decius nearly knocked her off her feet as he spun around, with a look of real fear on his face. He grabbed hold of her as she tumbled backward. "Salome, you caught me day dreaming."

"What frightful dream was that?"

Decius whispered in her ear, "Has any of your research in the synagogue foretold Jesus future?"

"We haven't had much time to spend on the Torah." Salome's suspicions grew. "What have you heard? Is Sextus worried?"

Decius changed the subject, slightly. "He's worried about controlling the crowds around Jesus in Jerusalem, because of the mob that descended on him at Peter's."

What was this man of hers keeping from her? "You and Sextus have become closer since Dorcas was healed."

"We have experienced the same overwhelming feelings of peaceful well-being." Decius walked beside her, keeping his eyes focused on the apostles and Jesus, who strolled before them. Then he glanced at her. "After the wedding in Cana, I thought you might want to set a date for marriage."

"Oh!" Salome jumped up and hugged his neck. The two Mary's behind them laughed. Salome waved at them and wove her arm around Decius's elbow. "Mary says two more years will be needed before she would approve our marriage. She did say she thinks you are a kind and good man." Salome knew the two women could hear her. "I wonder if I'll be taller in two years."

She let go of Decius's arm, but saddened to see his attention to Jesus and the apostles caused him to be unaware she released his arm. The two Mary approached her, each taking an elbow and walking her forward.

Magdalen said, "Men and their work, remind me of dogs on a scent."

Mary laughed. "My own son is too busy to remember his mother," she continued in a lighthearted tone, "and I was the one to teach him the commandments."

Salome compared the two women, who were both a head taller than she. Magdalen was wore red silk, her costume flowing as if made of individual veils; although her dress was modest enough, her uncovered, curly hair was adorned with golden pins and trinkets. Ide's ministrations before she danced for Herod came to Salome's mind. Where had all the golden bells and jade combs gone?

Mary, who wore a modest white robe and a blue head dressing and veil, asked her, "Salome, would you like to remove your veil and let the glorious crown of your curls wink at Decius?"

"Maybe later," Salome said, still dispirited by Decius's disinterest.

Magdalen searched under her numerous veils before pressing a small vial into Salome's hand. "When you expect to be alone with Decius, moisten the back of your ears with this ointment."

Mary nodded her approval.

Salome smelled the strong sent of roses. "Oh, my favorite." She hugged Magdalen and then included Mary in their embrace. "How would I survive without women friends?"

"How indeed," both answered.

*   *   *

Second Temple, Jerusalem

For the feast of Passover, the apostles and Decius followed Jesus as He went into the temple of God to worship. They were astonished when Jesus cast all those out that sold and bought in the temple. He knocked over the tables of the moneychangers and the chairs of those selling doves for sacrifice. Jesus would not allow any one to carry any vessel, be it wine or water, through the temple. Jesus raised His voice above the clamor He had instigated saying, "It is written, 'My house shall be called the house of prayer; but ye have made it a den of thieves!'"

Sextus and a large cohort of guards marched into the outer courtyard, as Decius and the apostles surrounded Jesus.

As Jesus descended the temple steps, there came to him the chief priests, and the scribes and the elders, and they said unto Him, "By what authority doest thou these things? And who gave thee this authority to do these things?

And Jesus answered and said unto them, "I will also ask of you one question, and answer me, and I will tell you by what authority I do these things. The baptism of John, was it from heaven, or of men? Answer me."

Decius heard them reasoning with themselves saying, "If we shall say, From heaven; he will say, Why then did ye not believe him? But if we shall say, of men, they feared the people: for all men counted John, that he was a prophet indeed. And they answered and said unto Jesus, "We cannot tell."

And Jesus answering saith unto them, "Neither do I tell you by what authority I do these things."

Decius nodded to Sextus, who moved his men between the priests and Jesus and the apostles. Without further incident or intimidation, the apostles and Jesus left Jerusalem heading for Jericho.

Chapter Seven

"Blessed are they which do hunger and thirst after
righteousness: for they shall be filled."

(Is 55:1; Matt 5:6)

River Jordan Route to Sea of Galilee

The trip back to Nazareth occupied the rest of the month of Nisan. Salome's memory of

the chariot ride with Decius in the first days of spring didn't compare to the tedious days of travel

walking north along the Jordan River. The arable river valley rich with flowering citrus trees

encouraged mosquitoes to worry their ears in the soft evenings.

Magdalen cautioned Salome not to use any perfumes while they were near the river.

"Men are not the only beings drawn to sweetness."

Salome wondered if the man she loved even knew she existed. Decius Invictus and

Sextus Orlando had stayed three extra days in Jericho so that Decius could copy down one of

Isaiah's scroll found in Jericho's synagogue. Mary had tried to persuade him that Nazareth's

synagogue would be made available, but Decius said the long trip home was an ideal time to

study the scripture. Salome searched her soul to see if she was envious of Decius reading in full

view of the other travelers. She longed to delve into the mysteries of holy words too; but Hebrew

traditions didn't allow such behavior for woman in public.

When Decius and Sextus caught up with them, the apostles and Jesus's brethren, Mary

sympathized with Salome's frustration. "Did you know the Hebrew word for a man's rib is

'Eve'?"

"Does that mean we are less than they?" Salome's anger nearly blotted out the sun.

Mary stroked her hand as they walked behind Decius and Sextus. "Less? How could God

want one creature to be better than another? I think our Creator made us from a man's rib to

show us how close we must be to a man, before we marry. . . almost as needful as his own rib."

"The commandments say we need to be under a husband's rule." Salome wasn't sure she

wanted to be ruled by a man who ignored her.

"That's to keep their fragile parts un-assailed," Magdalen said.

Mary shook her head. "I don't think Salome needs marital advice, right now. Husbands

do need to be informed and guided; but if they don't love us as they love themselves, or ask us to

commit some evil, we still must answer for our own souls."

Salome nodded her head. "Of course, the Lord knows our hearts."

Mary laughed. "Yes, even our unknown sins."

Salome wished she believed the way Decius and Sextus believed in Jesus. "Is it a sin not

to believe the way Decius does?"

"What does he believe?" Mary asked.

"That Jesus is the son of God, the Messiah," Salome said, then added, "who will forgive

our sins and bring heaven to earth."

Mary pulled Salome close to her. "Remember I told you about Elizabeth and me?"

Salome nodded, afraid to say aloud that Mary read the Torah with her cousin. "I taught Jesus all

the predictions about the Messiah's arrival, before we left him at the temple when he was twelve." Mary kept Salome's arm locked in hers. Her voice was low. "I assured Jesus that the

Messiah would have all the answers for the Hebrews to survive, even under Roman rule."

"How will he?"

"I don't know," Mary said. "But I believe my son, Jesus, does receive all he needs

directly from his Father in Heaven."

Salome wished her faith matched Mary's. But God knew her heart and Salome worried.

How could one learned rabbi change the mighty, military power of Rome into allowing a

peaceful life for the citizens under its rule? Romans couldn't even keep peace in their own royal

families, or at least not in hers.

*   *   *

On the Sea of Galilee

In Peter's large fishing vessel, Decius joined Salome on a boat bench facing the sunset.

He smiled, then kissed her brow before asking, "Remember when you first told me you were

reading the Torah for Mary?"

Salome checked to see if anyone was close enough to overhear their conversation. "I told

you in secret." Salome took his hand and placed her lips on his palm. "Because we will marry

someday soon."

"Do you remember what you found?"

Salome moved even closer for privacy. "Mary said her cousin Elizabeth first found the

verse after Mary visited her. Mary was with child. In 1 Samuel 2:34 it says, 'And this shall be a

sign unto you: Ye shall find the babe wrapped in swaddling clothes, lying in a manger."

"Does the Torah mention Bethlehem?"

"Oh yes, 'Genesis 49:10: And thou Bethlehem in the land of Judea, art not the least among the princes of Juda: for out of thee shall come a governor, that shall rule my people, Israel.'" As if remembering Decius was part of the Roman occupation, Salome was quick to add, "But Jesus says his kingdom is not of this world."

Decius followed the path of the sun as he mulled over her words. Then he rose and pulled her up to him, kissed her briefly, and set her apart from him before saying in a tone of great relief, "What better governor of our souls?"

"Have you spoken to Jacob about Jesus's baptism?"

Decius stood still, acknowledging the weight of the subject. "John baptized him."

"Jacob witnessed with his own eyes what Mary had read in Isaiah 61:1: 'I saw the Spirit descending from heaven like a dove and it abode upon Him.'"

Decius memorized her words, his lips moving over the sacred language. Then he placed his hand on the linen robe covering her shoulder, squeezing the cloth in case she missed the fact of their physical contact. "Jacob heard a voice, too. 'Behold my servant, whom I have chosen; my beloved, in whom my soul is well pleased: I will put my spirit upon Him, and He shall shew judgment to the Gentiles. He shall not strive, nor cry; neither shall any man hear His noise in the streets.'"

"Decius," Salome said, "Those are the words in Isaiah 42:2."

Decius was undeterred. "Jacob must have heard the verses speaking to him from his knowledge of the prophets."

*   *   *

Salome turned away from the view of the setting sun reflected in the Sea of Galilee. Her heart rose up in her when she saw Mary approach them. Mary would set Decius's faith on the right path. Salome trusted this woman even more than Decius, whom she loved with her whole heart. When Mary was close enough to hear, Salome called out, "Mary, come share the last shards of the sunset."

Mary sat down on the bench they had vacated. "Young love appreciates the world more than the rest of us."

Salome relaxed on the bench next to Mary. "Tell Decius the story of the old man, Simeon, who said he should not see death, before he had seen the Lord's Christ." Salome turned to Decius. "When she took Jesus to the temple for the first time as an infant."

Mary smiled at the tall Roman. "I was surprised to hear Simeon calling to the crowd. I was shy when I was younger. Simeon was very old. He had to raise his voice to be heard over the yammering of the multitude."

Decius turned his back on the glory of the purple and red clouds above the setting sun to listen to Mary.

"Simeon said, 'Behold this child is set for the fall and rising again of many in Israel: and for a sign which shall be spoken against.' Simeon came closer but his voice was still heard by those surrounding Joseph and me. 'Yea, a sword shall pierce through thy soul also, that the thoughts of many hearts may be revealed.' The old man took Jesus from my arms, held Him up and blessed God, and said, 'Lord, now lettest thou thy servant depart in peace, according to Thy word: for mine eyes have seen salvation, which thou as prepared before the face of all peoples; a light to lighten the Gentiles and the glory of the people of Israel.'"

"She kept all the words in her heart," Salome said to Decius.

Decius bowed his head. "I feel so privileged to be here, to know you." He laughed in real

delight. "and Salome."

Salome squeezed Mary's hand, as if to receive permission, before she leapt up and kissed

the man she would soon wed.

*   *   *

Capernaum, Iyar (Apr) 29 AD

When Jesus disembarked from Peter's boat at Capernaum, Decius assumed they would

gather again at Peter's compound. Instead, because of the large gathering, Jesus led the crowds

up the gentle slopes of a nearby mountain. Decius and Sextus, Salome, Magdalen and Mary, the

Mother of Jesus, sat as close to the rabbi as possible, just outside the circle of his disciples.

Jesus taught the crowds: "Blessed are the poor in spirit: for theirs is the kingdom of

heaven. Blessed are they that mourn: for they shall be comforted. Blessed are the meek for they

shall inherit the earth. Blessed are they which do hunger and thirst after righteousness for they

shall be filled. Blessed are the merciful for they shall obtain mercy. Blessed are the pure in heart

for they shall see God. Blessed are the peacemakers for they shall be called the children of God.

Blessed are they which are persecuted for righteousness sake for theirs is the kingdom of heaven.

Blessed are ye, when men shall revile you, and persecute you, and shall say all manner of evil

against you falsely, for my sake. Rejoice, and be exceeding glad for great is your reward in

heaven, for so persecuted they the prophets which were before you."

Decius was surprised to find during the long sermon that he would lose his concentration

and determination to memorize each word Jesus spoke.

Salome and Mary often turned to each other to acknowledge a phrase from the Torah. "Isaiah," Salome would say to Mary and Mary would nod.

Decius tried to ignore them to listen to Jesus.

"Think not that I am come to destroy the law, or the prophets: I am not come to destroy, but to fulfil."

Decius believed with all his heart, mind and soul that he was listening to the Son of God. He wished he was alone to hear every word; but the jostling crowd and his friends distracted him. Jesus's words swarmed around Decius. He wanted to catch each syllable, each nuance.

"…whosoever is angry with his brother without a cause shall be in danger of the judgment. Be reconciled to thy brother, and then come and offer thy gift before the altar."

Then Decius clearly heard, as a Roman occupier of Israel, what Jesus meant for him to pay attention to: "…resist not evil: but whosoever shall smite thee on they right cheek, turn to him the other also." Decius touched Sextus's shoulder to make sure his father's old friend was listening to this Jewish leader's words of peace. "Love your enemies, bless them that curse you, do good to them that hate you, and pray for them which despitefully use you and persecute you; That ye may be the children of your Father which is in heaven: for he maketh his sun to rise on the evil and on the good, and sendeth rain on the just and on the unjust. For if ye love them which love you, what reward have ye? Do not even the publicans the same? …Be ye therefore perfect, even as your Father which is in heaven is perfect."

When Decius heard the first words of the prayer Jesus taught him on the road from Machaerus, Decius knelt down next to Salome. He took her hand and they repeated the prayer with Jesus.

"Our Father which art in heaven, Hallowed be thy name. Thy kingdom come. Thy will be done in earth, as it is in heaven. Give us this day our daily bread. And forgive us our debts, as we forgive our debtors. And lead us not into temptation, but deliver us from evil: For thine is the kingdom, and the power, and the glory, for ever, Amen."

Salome kissed Decius's hand. He looked into her eyes. Here was his soul mate, but he recognized his faith in Jesus's salvation of his very soul differed from Salome's belief. Salome respected the rabbi, but she hadn't yet accepted Jesus as the Son of God. Decius couldn't find the words to convince the woman he wanted to marry. Her soul would need to ask for faith. Decius thanked the Lord he had received, as Sextus had, the great gift of faith. And Decius heard,

"…seek ye first the kingdom of God, and his righteousness; and all these things shall be added unto you. Take therefore no thought for the morrow: for the morrow shall take thought for the things of itself. Sufficient unto the day is the evil thereof."

Decius stood and looked over the surrounding crowd, wondering how many of Jesus's followers already believed in this walking miracle on earth. Did they understand the Son of God was speaking directly to them?

"Ask, and it shall be given you: seek, and ye shall find; knock, and it shall be opened unto you. Therefore whosoever heareth these sayings of mine, and doeth them, I will liken him unto a wise man, which built his house upon a rock: And the rain descended, and the floods came, and the winds blew, and beat upon that house; and it fell not: for it was founded upon a rock."

When Jesus finished speaking, He retired to Peter's compound in Capernaum.

*   *   *

Salome and the women, and Decius and Sextus, followed the disciples into Peter's compound. Mary's face was dark with worry. Salome thought she understood. Jesus's new teachings might help Israel citizens live more peacefully under Roman rule, but his notoriety would bring too much attention. Romans were jealous of their power: military, political and social and Pharisees worried the heels of the prophet.

Whispering just loud enough to be heard and challenging Jesus directly, these spies of the high priests in Jerusalem were no friends of his. "Why do you and your followers eat with sinners and tax-collecting publicans?'

Jesus answered, "They that be whole need not a physician, but they that are sick. But go ye and learn what that meaneth, 'I will have mercy, and not sacrifice: for I am not come to call the righteous, but sinners to repentance.'"

Among the group of women, one stooped with pain, pushed pass Salome.

Magdalen whispered, "I know her. For twelve years, she's been diseased with an issue of blood, unclean in the eyes of the priests; she's lost all her husband's savings paying doctors to restore her."

They watched as the woman came behind Jesus as he was waiting to see if the Pharisees would be brave enough to ask more questions. She touched the hem of his garment as if she believed even that touch could heal her.

Jesus turned about when he saw her, and said, "Daughter, be of good comfort, thy faith hath made thee whole."

When the woman rejoined their group, she told them she believed she was cured from that very hour. Mary and the other women agreed with her. Salome did too, believing the power of faith could cure or destroy people. She knew Decius and Sextus believed with the other women Jesus had healed the woman. But, Salome believed the woman saved herself. She wished

she could forget herself long enough to agree with the others; but she clung to her father Philip's

words, "The Lord knows our true thoughts."

She couldn't very well lie to Mary or Decius, so she decided to keep her own counsel,

unless asked.

*   *   *

Nazareth, Tammuz (Jun) 29 AD

Decius's world was at peace. Salome seemed to be growing along with the corn. Mary

had added a darker green hem to Salome's dress, which matched her modest veil. Even though

she was still a maid of fourteen, Salome acted as if her added height might convince everyone

she was old enough to become Decius's bride.

"I'm nearly 15. My birthday is in Tebeth, the same as the Lord's, doesn't that make a

difference?"

The dogs who matched each of Salome's changing moods seemed to agree with the

budding woman. Mary and Sextus shook their heads at each other. Decius held out his arms to

his beloved. "We are betrothed, Salome."

Salome's frown showed her disappointment and temper. "You find me wanting in belief,

isn't that the trutht?" Home who loved Salome to distraction began to howl. Nether tried to cheer

up the old dog, dancing around, bumping into him and getting nipped for her trouble. "Never

mind, never mind," Salome said to her pets. "Decius loves me. Someday he won't be able to

resist me."

Decius smiled at the child. If she knew half of the agony she put him through, she might

have more pity on his reticence.

Sextus noticed his quandary and rescued the situation. "Decius, I must speak to you at the station. Dear Mary, thank you for feeding us yet again. Dorcas insists you stop by to eat with us after one of your visits to the synagogue. She says she will only serve fresh fruit and cheese and bread."

Mary smiled. "Decius, enlighten this old friend of yours how scandalous a visit to an occupier's home would be for me."

"But you let us visit you," Sextus's feelings were injured.

Mary appealed with her hands to Decius.

Decius took his friend's arm, kissed Salome as they cleared the threshold and headed for Nazareth's police sentry house with Home following on their heels. "Mary's hospitality is legendary, Sextus. But the citizens of Nazareth are not happy with us."

"We are maintaining the peace." Sextus's pride refused to accept any guilt.

Decius kicked a loose flagstone to the edge of the road. "Why do you need to speak to me at the station?"

Sextus coughed. "A visitor, seeking evidence against my superior, dropped by."

"What has Rufus done now?" Decius asked, not really interested in the latest escapade of their drunken boss.

"There have been complaints, well really a speech of denunciation to the Roman Tribune…about Jesus."

"You know the Jewish priests want him stopped," Decius's tone sounded outraged even to his own ears. "Why would you believe such lies?"

"They are not lies." Sextus motioned for Decius to follow him into the lower floor of the building which served as their office. They could hear Dorcas moving around overhead in their living quarters. Sextus picked up a written report and read it to Decius, "A centurion says, 'Jesus disrupts the workers.'" Decius held up his hand to stop Sextus. But, Sextus ignored him continuing to read from the report, "'…as if the sun and spring distract them with joy and consolation.'"

"Faint praise," Decius said, "and dangerous if it reaches Rome. There is a curious power in Jesus's talks. He makes too real the teaching parables and people remember them as if they occurred in their own memories."

Sextus swept his hand in the air as if he need say no more.

*   *   *

Nazareth, Tishri (Sep) 29 AD

Salome spent every hour she could spare in Nazareth's synagogue with Mary searching for texts of Isaiah which they recognized in Jesus's Sermon on the Mount outside of Capernaum. "He does believe He can save us from the Romans."

"I am more afraid for Him now than I have ever been."

"I shouldn't have said 'from the Romans'." Salome tried to quiet any fear she might have instilled in Mary. "He's teaching everyone how to live under the Romans without causing strife. I don't know how many people will practice what He preaches."

"They need to believe in Him first."

Salome shook her head. "I believe He believes He knows the only way to live peacefully under the Romans, is that what you mean?"

"No." Mary turned to go. "Your heart will tell you, when you believe in Jesus, the way Decius, Sextus, and I do."

Salome dressed the scrolls and replaced them, before joining Mary. Why didn't they understand she did believe Jesus's words? The rabbi wasn't lying; she knew His integrity as well as she knew her own name. What was she missing that everyone alluded to but could not describe to her satisfaction? She shook her head, then repented, and sent a prayer to the Lord, "Lord, enlighten me in your way, Amen."

As Salome collected the dogs outside, now nearly the same size, she placed her hands on both their heads, relishing their loyalty. "You love me, don't you?"

Home looked into her eyes and licked her hand. Nether jumped about in his happy puppy fashion, although he was full grown, nearly knocking her down with his impulse to show his affection. "Down, Nether," she scolded. "You'll kill me before I'm old."

Decius appeared on the path as she rounded the gate to reach Mary's house. What a lovely man he'd become with his softer ways, his quiet tone, his loving eyes, the man had gentled into a more attractive male. When would he marry her? Decius seemed to read her thoughts, "Life of mine, have you settled the world's problems with Mary?"

"Only one remains," Salome tucked her arm under Decius's. "When will I be deemed worthy to marry you?"

"Ah," Decius said. "Sextus says our souls should not be unequally yoked."

Salome tried to control a rush of anger. She was after all a princess of the realm and Decius a mere household guard. True he was a Roman and the royal family of Israel was under Roman's rule; nevertheless, her royal blood superseded his family's line. She pulled her arm free.

Decius reacted to her changed mood. "Forgive me, Princess. Sextus was speaking of religious views only."

Salome drew a deep breath, trying to calm herself. If she wanted to be mature enough to marry, she'd need to control her emotions. The summer's decline left the air less humid. She listened to the grasshoppers singing their gratitude to the grain-laden fields about to be harvested. Decius's beard and hair were the same color as the stacked hay mounds. If he saw how long her hair had grown, he might find her attractive enough to marry.

Decius spoke softly, "Salome, I was predisposed to belief in Jesus. Seeing the way your people live their religion as opposed to examples I witnessed in Rome, I was seeking the truth. When I met Jesus alone on the road from Machaerus, desperate to find you, I experienced the peace surrounding Him. I know it sounds crazy, if not unusual but Jesus is my closest friend, as if He knows my needs before I do. I trust Him with my soul. See, you haven't been able to want for a God. You believe in the God of Abraham."

Salome eyed this man she desired to catch. "I could lie to you."

"I trust you." Decius dismissed the subject. "How does Mary feel about Jesus latest sermon?"

"She's frightened for His very life." Salome said, hushing herself as they entered Mary's house.

Decius bowed to Mary, pointed at Sextus, and told her, "While we yet live, you have nothing to fear about the safety of your son."

Salome didn't see the shift in worry she expected to read on Mary's face. Instead Mary said, "Let's bless our food before we eat."

During the next several weeks, Salome kept a close watch over Mary. In fact, Mary's daughters noticed, asked Salome if anything was wrong. Salome blushed to realize she'd been so obvious. "No, no. I'd just like to help out more. Is there anything else I could do?"

Anne, the youngest daughter-in-law, laughed. "My children seem to gather energy with this colder weather. They're wearing me out. I've been coming later and later in the morning to help Mary dress her hair. Since you're already here, could you take over? I'll sweep the walk at night before supper in trade, the laundry, or walk your dogs?"

Salome was relieved. "If you sweep up, that would be a fair trade. Home and Nether's hearts would break if I didn't go for a walk with them."

So every morning, Salome helped the mother of Jesus comb her long, soft tresses before the day began. Salome's own red curls grew past her shoulders finally, but she kept them tied at the nape of her neck so they wouldn't creep out from under her veil. Mary's hair fell past her waist and Salome helped to braid and twist the hair into a comfortable style, also hidden by Mary's blue veil.

Mary's burden of worry hadn't lifted since the Sermon on the Mount. She and Salome prayed in Nazareth's synagogue more than they searched the scriptures, now. Salome noticed more and more of Mary's dark brown hair was turning a transparent white from worry.

And then one day after Yom Kippur, Salome noticed a change. Mary seemed taller, her eyes brighter. Salome couldn't help but comment. "What has changed, Mother?"

Mary reached up and grasped Salome's hand as she brushed her hair. "I asked the Lord to take care of my son, every day; and then finally, I prayed for strength to let go of worry, to trust God more." Mary turned and faced Salome. "I'm not saying everything will be fine for my son. God has great plans for Jesus and I fear for His life, but I now believe I'll be able to find the strength to stay by His side. I'm so happy, can you tell?"

Salome nodded her head. She knew in her heart she would not be able to accept the death of any of her children. Parents were supposed to outlive their children in the natural order of things. As she continued to dress Mary's hair, she realized Mary's courage far exceeded the bravery of anyone she had ever known.

Herodias came to mind. Hateful was the only word that applied to her mother, self-centered, greedy…there were a few more. "Mary?" Salome asked, "Do you think I need to repent for abandoning my mother?"

"As I understand the situation, you were well out of the palace, but you could let your mother know you forgive her, even if you don't condone her actions."

"Really? That doesn't sound like forgiveness to me."

"The Lord doesn't expect us to turn a blind eye to the faults of others. We're only required to keep our hearts open, in case they need us."

"When we go to Jerusalem for Passover," Salome suddenly felt a strong pull to see her mother. "I could slip into the palace."

"Decius will help you, won't he?"

"It might be too dangerous for Decius, but Sextus could help."

"I'll pray for you," Mary said.

And Salome was heartened, here was the Mother of Jesus imploring the Lord for help. Surely, all would go well.

One day late in the season, Salome watched the harvest workers coming home from a day in the fields along the pathways surrounding Nazareth. Nether no longer needed her leash, Decius was at her side, and Home trailed closely behind.

Decius's attention was drawn to a group of bareheaded young girls, walking with their arms locked together. "Women are just more beautiful than men," he said, smiling at Salome.

"You need to marry, Decius." Salome's heart sank. "How old are you?"

"Twenty, Salome." He squeezed her hand. "Don't play, now."

"Play!" She stomped her sandal on the street. Home barked a warning and Nether's ears flattened. "Now see what you've done." Salome bent down to pet her companions. "They don't understand." She stood up abruptly knocking into his shoulder. "And I don't either." Decius reached for her. Salome suddenly remembered when her hair caught in his leather bracing long ago in the Machaerus castle. "You saved me once; can't you marry me now?"

"I will, I promise." Decius held her forearm as if afraid she would run. He whispered, "Princess, you know you are the only woman I love."

"Someday," Salome said, knowing her pouting mood was showing. "But not now. You might as well go home. I'll see you tomorrow."

She watched Decius obey. He walked dejectedly, as if he didn't own a friend in the world. The tall Roman, wearing Mary's signature seamless robe, passed through Nazareth's gate on his sorry way to the sentry house. Salome couldn't let him suffer. She ran after him, not caring what the girls in the lane thought of her. "Decius," she called.

Decius stopped and ran back towards her. "I love you more than I can breathe."

"I am sorry," Salome said. "I'm just so frustrated. I wish I could tell you I believe the same way the rest of you do about Jesus." She kissed his cheek. "I've been praying for faith."

"The Lord will answer, Salome," Decius said. "But in the meantime don't worry. We have each other."

She snuggled against him for a moment breathing in his scent, devouring his warmth, and then she returned to Mary's house.

The flowers in the window boxes and along the path to the house needed watering, as did her soul. Or maybe they didn't have enough sun this late in the season. Now close to 15, she knew marriage was still ahead of her, still blooming in her future.

Chapter Eight

"I will open my mouth in parables; I will utter
things which have been kept secret from the
foundation of the world.
                                        (Ps 78-2: Matt 13:37-52)

Capernaum, Tabeth (Dec) 29 AD

Decius followed Jesus as he left Peter's compound to sit by the seaside. Even before the

sun was fully risen, crowds found their rabbi. Peter suggested Jesus make use of his fishing boat

to address the people on the shore. Salome and Mary joined Decius to listen.

"His birthday is in a few days," Mary told Salome.

"Mine, too." Salome smiled at Decius as if to claim the significance.

Jesus spoke of many things in parables. "Behold, a sower went forth to sow; And when

he sowed, some seeds fell by the way side, and the fowls came and devoured them up: Some fell

upon stony places, where they had not much earth: and forthwith they sprung up, because they

had no deepness of earth: And when the sun was up, they were scorched; and because they had

no root, they withered away. And some fell among thorns; and the thorns sprung up, and choked

them: But others fell into good ground, and brought forth fruit, some an hundredfold, some

sixtyfold, some thirtyfold. Who hath ears to hear, let him hear."

After Jesus sent the multitude away and returned to Peter's house. His disciples came to the evening repast, too. John asked, speaking for the rest of the disciples, "Declare unto us the parable of the tares of the field."

Jesus answered, "He that soweth the good seed is the Son of man; the field is the world, the good seed are the children of the kingdom; but the tares are the children of the wicked. The enemy that sowed them is wicked; the harvest is the end of the world; and the reapers are the angels. As therefore the tares are gathered and burned in the fire; so shall it be in the end of this world. The son of man shall send forth his angels, and they shall gather out of his kingdom all things that offend, and them which do iniquity; And shall cast them into a furnace of fire: there shall be wailing and gnashing of teeth. Then shall the righteous shine forth as the sun in the kingdom of their Father." Jesus said unto them, "Have you understood all these things?"

They answered him, "Yea, Lord."

*   *   *

In the cooking compound attached to the dining quarters, Salome sought out Mary, who was rolling out honey-and-date cakes, a favorite of her son's. "Mary, do you remember Psalm 78?" Salome asked, helping to load the stone oven with the fragrant pastries.

Mary was quick to quote, "I will open my mouth in parables; I will utter things which have been kept secret from the foundation of the world."

"I knew you were thinking those words as we listened." Salome's ears itched from the heat of the ovens. She laughed. 'I believe faith is prickling my ears."

Mary laughed, too. Then she came over to Salome, put her arms around her and hugged her tight. "I know you will believe some day. The trouble is your father's words still ring in your ears and you're afraid to lose them."

Salome began to cry. "You know my heart."

"It is a good heart, Salome." Mary returned to her birthday preparations.

And Salome? She retained the comfort of her familiar doubts.

*   *   *

Gergesenes Tabeth (Dec) 29 AD

Decius had watched Jesus and his disciples enter Peter's ship to pass over to the eastern shore of Galilee. Gergesenes was an unholy place even in the eyes of the Romans. Later the same day when the boat returned, Thomas jumped off the ship first. Decius helped him moor the boat to the dock.

"I need to talk," Thomas said. He turned and without saying a word to his fellow disciples strolled off in the opposite direction from Peter's compound.

Decius walked next to him. "What is it?" Of all the apostles, Thomas seemed the closest to Decius in his beliefs and awareness of a wider world.

"I may be following a magician." Thomas stopped in his tracks. He bent over with his hands on his knees. "Surely, not."

Decius guided him to a low stonewall, out of view of the docks. "Explain why you are so upset."

"Salome needs to hear this. I know you have been pressuring her to believe. I need to tell her the facts."

"Stay here," Decius said. Somehow he knew Salome shouldn't hear one word from Thomas, but he also knew Thomas had a right to voice his doubts. "I'll be right back. Are you hungry?"

Thomas's stomach growled in response. Decius called over his shoulder, "Wait for me."

Decius ran in the direction of Peter's compound. The rest of the disciples and Jesus acted as if they were in a state of shock. The eleven men dragged their feet and appeared strangely unfocused. Jesus was still standing next to the boat, gazing across the sea toward its eastern shoreline.

"Salome," Decius called as he approached the cooking shed.

She was immediately in his arms, her face close to his. "What do you want, you silly man?"

Decius was surprised when he sort of shook her. Her face changed from a glad welcome to surprise and a hint of anger. "Please, Salome, Thomas says he must speak to you. I'm worried. He's hungry." He couldn't explain his fear. Then he knew. Fear was not from God. Something evil was afoot. "Don't let Mary know where we're going."

"I never lie to Mary." Salome shook her head. He watched as she shoved a loaf of bread, a wine flask and a few pieces of onion and cheese into a traveling satchel. Without saying goodbye to Mary, she swiftly joined Decius at the door.

When they reached Thomas, he was sobbing. Decius forced a sip of wine down him before Thomas became aware Salome was with Decius. "Princess," he said.

"Hush," Salome cautioned. "Who told you?"

"We all know," Thomas said. "It doesn't matter, but I'm glad you could come to hear this." Thomas swallowed more wine from the flask, before starting his tale. "When we arrived in

Gergesenes, there met us two possessed, coming down the mountain out of the tombs. We were told they were exceeding fierce, so violent that no one could pass by that way. One had been bound with leather fetters and chains, and the chains had been plucked asunder by him, and the fetters broken to pieces. The trailing chains and fetters hung from his shoulders and waist. The other man shouted day and night from the tombs, cutting himself with stones." Thomas chewed thoughtfully on a bit of bread before continuing, "Neither of them wore any clothing. When they saw us, both of them cried out saying, 'What have we to do with thee, Jesus, thou Son of God? Art thou come hither to torment us before the time?' And there was a good way off from them an herd of many swine feeding."

"And Jesus said, 'Come out of the men, thou unclean spirits.' And Jesus asked them, 'What is thy name?'"

"They answered, 'Legion: for we are many.' And they besought Him that He would not send them away out of the country. And all the evil spirits besought Him saying, 'Send us into the swine that we may enter into them.' And when they were come out, they went into the herd of swine. The whole herd of swine of about two thousand ran violently down a steep place into the sea and perished in the waters."

Decius looked at Salome. She was shaking her head in disbelief.

Thomas continued, "And the people that fed the swine fled, and went different ways into the city, and told everything...what had taken place. And the whole city came out to meet Jesus. They saw the two men who had been possessed sitting at the feet of the Lord and clothed, and in their right mind. They became frightened of us and asked us to leave their coasts. The men who had been ill begged to be taken into the ship with us."

"But Jesus said, 'Go home to thy friends, and tell them how great things the Lord hath done for thee, and hath had compassion on thee.'"

Salome was the first to speak. "Thomas, if you believe Jesus is the personification of good…" Here Thomas nodded his head, yes. His mouth was full of bread and cheese. "…then I can understand why you might believe people can contain evil spirits."

Decius was nodding assent along with Thomas.

"Don't you, Salome, after your own mother…," Thomas could not find words to explain the exploitation of the woman's only daughter.

"I believe in the person of God," Salome said. "However, I think the evil that we do is sufficient harm. I think we should take responsibility for our actions and not blame them on a third entity."

"Else we are not ethically able to claim any moral high ground?" Thomas was pulling on his dark beard. "But I saw…"

"A remarkable coincidence." Salome patted Decius on his shoulder, as if to comfort him, too. "Loud men were shouting and rattling their chains, making a commotion. The herd of pigs stampeded into the sea in fright. I need to help Mary feed this army of do-gooders." She laughed and strolled away.

Decius felt he was worse off, more at sea about his beliefs, than Thomas. "It's getting dark," he said. "Let's join the others."

"But, Decius, even though, I'm not sure what happened in Gergesenes, I think Peter and Mary are right. See how easily Salome was able to explain away this miracle. If you marry her now, you might lose your faith."

Decius was already worried. "Why would a Messiah be needed to redeem us, if we take responsibility for our own evil?"

"See, you are already being led astray."

But Decius felt assured. Jesus was the only way to truth...whatever the cost...whatever the truth. He understood that Salome found a logical explanation for the scene Thomas had described in Gergesenes. What he didn't comprehend was the dissonance Thomas seemed to be experiencing. On the one hand, he cautioned against marrying an unbeliever, on the other hand Thomas obviously had doubts about the miracle of driving evil spirits into a herd of pigs, which destroyed themselves. Decius's ethics wondered how Jesus justified the destruction of those poor farmers' property. No wonder the apostles were asked to leave, even if they had restored two of their citizens to good health. He was assured Thomas believed the Lord's way was the only true path to follow.

Decius, however, did agree with Salome on one point: saying the devil made someone do something took away the responsibility of committing the sin. The redemption Jesus promised didn't negate individual will power, else how could they ask for the Lord's help, his forgiveness. But for Decius, his belief did promise a more peaceful way to live, a right direction. Perhaps he would never become as pure of sin as he wished, but he was willing to follow God's will, not his own.

*   *   *

Magdala, Tabeth (Jan) 30 AD

Salome had looked forward to visiting Magdalen in her home town of Magdala. She wanted to see what all the colorful mystery was about. Of course, Salome knew Magdalen was considered a woman of ill repute. But if the mother of Jesus found the friendly, humorous woman fit company, Salome felt her own tenuous position in society, as a run-away royal, was as

much of a problem as Magdalen's for Mary.

The winter winds on the Sea of Galilee had been chilling. Decius had given Salome a fur-

lined cloak for her birthday. She'd wanted a wedding, but today she was thankful for the warmth

of the thoughtful gift. Sextus had made some convenient excuse to man the sentry station in

Nazareth, freeing Decius to accompany Salome and Mary on the trip to Magdala.

Magdalen did not meet them at the shore, but the apostles seemed to know the way to her

house. Salome first glimpsed Magdala through a heavy snowfall.

"The snow flakes are sticking to your eyelashes." Decius came close enough for a kiss, so

Salome jumped up, meaning to kiss his cheek; but he caught her by the waist, pulling her close

for a sweet kiss on her lips.

"Much better," she said.

"Careful, children," Mary cautioned. "The walk is slippery."

Gray towers, as high as two houses, dotted the landscape. The tall fish-drying equipment

behind most of the homes of fishermen stood out in stark relief against the snow-covered hills

surrounding Magdala. Salome expected to smell the fish, but the cold kept any repugnant odors

from reaching them. Large pieces of snow continued to fall, creating a shifting white curtain

before the town. Closest to the shore, a domed house of at least three floors rose above them. Its

windows glowed red from fires or lanterns. As they approached, the front door opened and a blue

turbaned servant ushered them in.

A huge fireplace faced the door and the warmth from the mammoth hearth welcomed the

group. The servant directed them to sit on the benches on each side of the entranceway. Beautiful

unveiled maidens offered to wash their feet with warm water and towels.

Magdalen went directly to Jesus. She carried an alabaster box of ointment. At first she stood behind his bench weeping, then she began to wash his feet with her tears and wiped them with the ointment.

Salome relished the rose scent filling the entranceway from the salve, but her attention was drawn away by the jangling sound of Judas Iscariot's purse as he turned to whisper to Thomas. "Surely Jesus knoweth what manner of woman this is that toucheth him, for she is a sinner."

And Jesus answered saying unto Simon, "I have somewhat to say unto thee. There was a certain creditor which had two debtors: the one owed five hundred pence and the other fifty. And when they had nothing to pay, he frankly forgave them both. Tell me therefore, which of them will love him most?'

Simon answered, "I suppose that he, to whom he forgave most."

And Jesus said unto him, "Thou hast rightly judged." And he turned to Magdalen and said, "Simon, seest thou this woman? I entered into thine house, thou gavest me no water for my feet: but she hath washed my feet with tears and wiped them with the hairs of her head. Thou gavest me no kiss: but this woman since the time I came in hath not ceased to kiss my feet. My head with oil thou didst not anoint: but this woman hath anointed my feet with ointment. Wherefore I say unto thee. Her sins, which are many, are forgiven; for she loved much but to whom little is forgiven, the same loveth little."And he turned again to Magdalen and said, "Thy sins are forgiven. Thy faith hath saved thee; go in peace."

Mary, the mother of Jesus, motioned for Salome to follow her. Mary embraced Magdalen and led her up a staircase next to the fireplace. Salome nodded first to Decius and then withdrew with the two women.

Magdalen's room was on the top floor. Its domed ceiling was painted a bright blue. The whitewashed walls, white bedstead and tables as well as the snowy bedding and bed hangings resembled a bridal chamber, more than a seductive lair. The air was filled with the heady smell of roses. Salome searched the room for actual blooms before realizing Magdalen's perfume was the cause of the pleasant sweet smell. A yellowish brightness from rounded windows of thin alabaster sheets framed in blue mosaic tile added to the wholesomeness of the place. The fireplace was guarded with a matching screen of alabaster-and-blue mosaic tiles.

"You must break with your old life, Magdalen." Mary seemed un-impressed with the luxury of the room. "We'll take you to your sister and brother in Jericho."

"Lazarus won't allow me in his house." Magdalen valiantly tried to stop her weeping. "And Martha will not go against his wishes."

"My son will intervene," Mary said.

"Who will take care of my servants?" Magdalen twisted a strand if her long red hair.

"First, Magdalen," Mary said softly, "We must ensure your soul's survival. The servants will be taken care of. Matthew will see to the distribution of your fortune. Now we must find a quiet respite for you to regain your balance."

Salome stood by, waiting to be of some assistance. "Shall I bring water, Mother?"

"Yes," Mary said. "Ask the maids to prepare a bath for Magdalen."

Salome returned as quickly as possible not wanting to miss any of Mary's words of wisdom. Mary was still speaking quietly, and Salome needed to concentrate away from the bustle of the maids to hear every word. "When you touch another person," Mary was saying, "all of their world is affected by you. Their family, friends, people they work with, their acquaintances at the synagogue, all become entwined with your life. That's true for me, for Salome, for anyone.

People are too precious to use for any purpose. We must honor each other's souls, so that when

we meet our maker we can honestly say, we have harmed no one."

"I cannot say that." Magdalen sobbed.

Salome caressed her friend. "That's all in the past, now."

"We all have time to change." Mary's voice shifted slightly. "Now, pack as little as

possible."

"Do you need my help, Mother?" Salome asked, wanting to rejoin Decius. Mary smiled

and waved her away.

As Salome re-entered the main entrance, she gasped at what she saw.

Jesus had laid aside his white robe and girded himself with a towel. He'd taken one of the

basins from a servant and poured in warm water from the heated jars near the fireplace. Jesus

knelt down and began to wash his apostles' feet, and to wipe them with the towel wherewith he

was girded.

When he reached Peter's feet, Peter said, "Lord, dost thou wash my feet?"

Jesus answered, "What I do thou knowest not now; but thou shalt know hereafter."

Peter argued with him, "Thou shalt never wash my feet."

Jesus said, "If I wash thee not, thou hast no part with me."

So Peter said, "Lord, not my feet only, but also my hands and my head."

And Jesus said, "He that is washed needeth not save to wash his feet, but is clean every

whit: and ye are clean, but not all." Jesus looked at Judas Iscariot and said, "Ye are not all clean."

When Decius, the apostles and Jesus were seated at the table for their evening repast,

Salome joined the serving girls. Mary and Magdalen did not join them. Salome was almost too

busy to hear all of Jesus's words, but she tried to listen to the learned rabbi.

"Verily, verily, I say unto you, The servant is not greater than his lord; neither he that is sent greater than he that sent him. He that receiveth whomsoever I send receiveth me; and he that receiveth me receiveth him that sent me."

Salome heard the words, but couldn't see how they applied to her life. She chanted the 23rd Psalm to herself as she helped clean up after the meal. Each word held meaning for her, capped her emotions with reason, stayed her fears, guided her actions, and promised eternal peace.

*   *   *

After the evening meal, Decius wandered around Magdalen's house. Most of the chamber doors were left open, because fireplaces at each end of the halls heated the rooms. Decius counted thirteen rooms. He found Thomas standing in a whitewashed room with an elaborate wall sketch of blue chalk, showing a temple of some kind reflected in a blue pond.

Thomas explained the sketch. "Magdalen said a king from the east brought his twelve-year-old son here to learn the ways of women. In their land they arrange the marriage of their children nearly at birth. The boy refused to touch any of the women saying he was in love with his wife. The king left him here for a month, but the only thing the boy accomplished was this striking drawing. He said he or his sons would build this palace for his wife. I'd like to take the message of the Lord to his kingdom, where love is already so strong."

In the room next door, Decius found John and James Boarnerges, the sons of thunder, arguing loudly over who would lay claim to one heavily embroidered coat lined with sheepskin. They had strewn clothes out of the closet onto the bed and floor, in their attempt to find warmer clothes.

Decius heard Andrew, Peter's brother, speaking in Greek to Philip in the next room. Peter was standing in the doorway with his huge arms stretched up to the lintel. He looked as if he was ready to pull the house down. Judas Iscariot was sitting at a huge desk facing the doorway of another room. His head was in his hands, with his elbows propped on the desk filled with stacks of gold coins.

Matthew excused himself and walked past Decius into the room. "Just give her coffers to the poor," Matthew said.

"And, you, a tax collector," Judas said. He recognized Decius, a Roman, was listening, too. "What will the authorities think of these sin-begotten monies? Will good come from them?"

Decius answered as he thought the rabbi might, "Stones cannot sin. The money will help many find food today." As he left to further investigate Magdalen's home, he wondered if he should have brought up the cache of money behind Peter's dining hall, which he had seen Judas bury. Somehow he couldn't bring himself to confront the man. If Matthew had not been in the room, Decius thought he might have questioned the money-handler.

He found the rest of the apostles, Bartholomew, Janus Thaddaeus, Jude, and Simon, laying out pallets for the evening's stay. Planning to speak with Salome, he returned to the main floor. Now that Salome had turned fifteen, Decius hoped Mary would find a way for them to be together, even if Salome had yet to believe Jesus was sent to save them from their sins.

Jesus stood looking into the fire. Decius rushed across the room to embrace Salome as she came down the steps. Jesus turned towards them with a gentle smile on His face.

Salome boldly asked Him, "Rabbi, is it wrong for us to want to marry. Decius believes in you; but I still honor my father's beliefs."

Jesus put his hand on Decius's shoulder, but looked into Salome's soul as he answered, "Whosoever shall give to drink unto one of these…a cup of cold water only, in the name of a disciple, verily I say unto you, she shall in no wise lose her reward."

Decius thought Salome was going to jump into his arms; but instead she rushed up the staircase to tell Mary her glad news.

*   *   *

Salome burst into Magdalen's room. "Jesus says Decius and I can be married."

Mary dropped a basket filled with Magdalen's reduced wardrobe. "Nevertheless."

Magdalen dried her tears. "My brother, Lazarus, would be happy to host the wedding, Mary."

Mary's laughter eased Salome's soul back to its rejoicing track. "In Jericho." Then Salome remembered her friend, Ide. "Could I invite the parents of my friend, who lived in Jericho?" Salome stifled a sob. "Ide died when Decius and I traveled to Nazareth."

Mary and Magdalen were quick to embrace Salome. Magdalen said, "You can invite all of Jericho."

Mary excused herself. "Let me speak to my son and Decius."

*   *   *

Decius had to agree with Mary; Salome's aging father should be asked to approve Salome's marriage to a Roman. Decius then asked for Jesus's guidance. Caesarea Philippi, the capitol of Philip's Tetrarchy, was at the northern most point of Canaan, one source of the Jordan

River. Thomas was summoned and agreed to accompany Mary, Magdalen, and Salome to Jericho while the disciples, Decius and Jesus traveled to Caesarea Philippi.

*   *   *

On the road to Jericho, 30 AD

Thomas Didymus argued about Jesus's mission on earth all the way to Jericho. Out of politeness, Salome mostly agreed with his opinions of universal love; even though Decius's beliefs held a more sweeping view of the benefits of complete faith in his rabbi's teachings of redemption. Mary and Magdalen took issue with Thomas's views, too.

Thomas quoted Jesus often; but none of the women had heard Jesus speak in the same vein. "Jesus told me," Thomas said, "'If you bring forth what is within you, what you bring forth will save you. If you do not bring forth what is within you, what you do not bring forth will destroy you.'"

"Decius does not believe Jesus came only as a guide to open access to our spiritual understanding." Salome hoped Mary or Magdalen would voice their agreement, but the two women didn't break their stride over the chaff-packed paths on the side of the muddied and rutted road which required their full attention.

Thomas insisted, "He said, 'I am not your master. Because you have drunk, you have become drunk from the bubbling stream which I have measured out. He who will drink from my mouth will become as I am: I myself shall become he, and the things that are hidden will be revealed to him.'"

"Why did Jesus tell only you these things?" Salome asked.

"Oh, not only me," Thomas said. "Jesus told the sons of Thunder, John and James, 'Ye know that they which are accounted to rule over the Gentiles exercise lordship over them; and their great ones exercise authority upon them. But so shall it *not* be among you: but whosoever will be great among you, shall be your minister; and whosoever of you will be the chiefest, shall be servant of all. For even the Son of man came not to be ministered unto, but to minister, and to give His life a ransom for many.'"

Mary stopped ahead of them. Magdalen took a step or two before she, too, ceased to walk. Salome skipped ahead of them to face the mother of Jesus. "He is giving His life to teach us His ways, Mother."

"Yes," Mary said, too quietly.

Salome knew the word 'ransom' was a frightening thing to hear in connection with Mary's son. "Surely, the Lord will protect our rabbi."

Mary and Magdalen resumed the journey. Salome skipped backward before them for a bit, trying in vain to think of something to cheer the two.

Thomas seemed unaware of the havoc he was creating. "Jesus told me, 'Since it has been said that you are my twin and true companion, examine yourself so that you may understand who you are...I am the knowledge of the truth. So while you accompany me; although you do not understand, you already have come to know, and you will be called: the one who knows himself...For whoever has not known himself has known nothing, but whoever has known himself has simultaneously achieved knowledge about the depth of things.'"

Salome seriously considered Thomas's words. "You are saying that whoever receives the spirit communicates directly with the divine?"

"Yes!" Thomas thumped Salome's back. "Jesus told me, 'If the spirit came into being because of the body, it is a wonder of wonders, Indeed, I am amazed at how this great wealth (the spirit) has made its home in this poverty (the body).'"

Mary turned and addressed them, "The Kingdom of God is not of this world, it is a spiritual Kingdom."

Salome sounded the depths of her soul. God was present. "He restoreth my soul," she quoted from her favorite Psalm.

Magdalen added the verse, "He leadeth me in paths of righteousness for His Name's sake."

Thomas seemed gladdened with what he perceived was their agreement. "Jesus told me, also that, 'Look, (if) the Kingdom is in the sky; then the birds will arrive before you. If they say to you: It is in the sea; then he says the fish will arrive before you. Instead it is a state of inner discovery. ...Rather the Kingdom is inside of you, and it is outside of you. When you come to know yourselves, then you will be known, and you will realize that you are the children of the living Father. But if you will not know yourselves, then you dwell in poverty, and it is you who are that poverty.'"

As they reached Lazarus's home, Mary quoted a Psalm that voiced their common belief as a greeting to Magdalen's brother and sister, Lazarus and Martha, "Truth has sprung forth from the earth."

*   *   *

Caesarea Philippi, 30 AD

Decius shed the robe Mary had woven for him in order to present himself as a Roman soldier in Philip's palace. Decius had not meant to conceal Salome's name, merely stating that he carried news from the family in order to gain entrance. Without too much delay, Decius was

allowed a private audience with the Tetrarch. Decius was surprised at the age of the ruler, who

seemed shrunken, even frail, under his royal robe of purple and gold.

"Which of my family has sent you?" Philip asked.

"I hesitate to mention the name," Decius stated truthfully.

Philip smiled slightly. "So you, too, have heard Tiberius's words, '...that it is safer to be

Herod's pig than his son.'"

Decius bowed in response. "It is a daughter of the realm, that I come to discuss."

"To discuss?" Philip frowned. "My wife?"

"No, Sire." Decius went down on one knee, as he had before this man's wife, Herodias,

on the fateful day he fell deeply in love. He cleared his dry throat. "The hand of your daughter,

Salome."

Philip leapt to his feet. "She's alive?"

"Hidden, my Lord."

"Safe." Philip said, retaking the throne seat. "I've prayed unceasingly..."

"You taught her well." Decius stood. "She prays night and day, as she promised you."

Philip eyed him thoughtfully. "I heard you say you wanted to marry my only daughter.

She's much too young. Thirteen?"

"Fifteen, Lord."

"I take it you have already asked her?" Philips eyes bore into Decius, as if trying to read

his every thought. "How did you come upon her?"

"I rescued her the night...that John the Baptist..."

"Was beheaded at the request of my wife?" Philip didn't blink.

"I took her to a safe haven. A woman in Nazareth, named Mary, takes in strangers."

"She obviously didn't know who my daughter was." Philip drew his cloak around him as if suddenly chilled by the hatred of his people.

"Actually, we were surprised she did know your daughter and welcomed her into her home." Decius's mind searched for something more to say in the gathering silence descending on their conversation. "Salome reads for Mary in Nazareth's synagogue, because you were wise enough to teach your brilliant daughter to not only love the holy words but to read them as well." Again Decius searched the silence for more to say. "Salome has two pets, a sheepdog and a black hound she calls 'Nether.' The sheepdog was already named 'Home.' Salome has grown from here to here." Decius measured off the straps of his breastplate, remembering how she had first caught her hair. "To hide Salome's identity, we cut her beautiful red hair when we fled with one of her maids, Ide, who died during the journey; but Mary says Salome's hair has grown past her shoulders. I haven't seen it because she wears a Jewish veil. Mary weaves seamless robes for her."

"Stop talking," Philip said with his hand raised in protest. "Let me think."

Decius stopped speaking for a long minute. "You'll want to know of my parents. They're both dead. Invictus was their name. A friend of my father's, Sextus Orlando, helped Salome and me."

Philip frowned.

"I haven't touched your daughter," Decius stuttered, "I…I mean I've kissed her and hugged her not too much, just in greeting, or saying good-night. She sleeps in Mary's house. Sextus and I man the sentry station in Nazareth. We have a housekeeper, Dorcas."

"Stop talking." Philip stood.

Decius ceased to speak.

The Tetrarch, who was a head shorter than Decius, swept past him. He motioned for him to follow as he stepped out onto a large veranda. "We will less likely be overheard by spies in my household," Philip explained.

"Of course," Decius said, well aware of royal courts intrigues. "How may I serve you?"

"Marry my daughter," Philip took off five of his costly rings. "Consider this her dowry. I'll endanger both your lives, if I ask to see her."

"She knows you love her…." Decius tried to assure Salome's father, who was close to weeping. "…more than anything in your life,"

"Tell her to love the Lord," Philip said. Then a twinkle in his eye made Decius realize where Salome inherited her good nature. Philip added, "…more than you Decius, such a handsome Roman man for my daughter to choose. Your children will be beautiful. Have as many as the Lord wills."

Decius began to weep. "Sorry, Sire…I…"

"You need her love as much as she needs yours," Philip said, raising his hand to place it on Decius's shoulder. "You have my blessings. May God protect us all."

Decius left the palace, joyful he had received Philip's permission to marry Salome but saddened, too, by the likelihood neither of them would be able to visit Philip, openly.

He rejoined the apostles on the edge of Tetrarch Philip's city of Caesarea Philippi where Jesus walked among the poor and hungry. Peter and Andrew cleared a path for their rabbi through the surging crowds. Philip and Matthew followed close behind Jesus, as if they were appointed, watchful guards to royalty. Cheerful Bartholomew, faithful Janus Thaddaeus, the Canaanite Simon and young Jude mingled among the people. The shorter Boarnerges, John and

James, were quickly swallowed up in the mass of tattered folk, who were relegated to live in shacks outside the city because of sickness, or estrangement from their family for religions reasons, or crushing poverty.

Decius joined Judas Iscariot, who was taking in the scene from a slight rise above the flow of people. "I can smell them from here," Judas said.

"Jesus loves them all," Decius said.

Judas turned and eyed Decius defiantly. "But he loves us more."

"Does love have boundaries? Can it be weighed or metered out?" Decius watched as Jesus separated himself from the crowd below and walked toward them.

His disciples followed in quick order. When they had gathered about Him, Jesus asked them, "Whom do men say that I am?"

Some answered in unison, "John the Baptist."

But others of the group said, "Elias."

Judas raised his voice. "One of the prophets."

And He said to them, "But whom say ye that I am?"

And Peter answered, "Thou art the Christ.

"Blessed art thou, …for flesh and blood hath not revealed it unto thee, but my Father which is in heaven. And I say also unto thee, That thou art Peter, and on this rock I will build my church; and the gates of hell shall not prevail against it. And I will give unto thee the keys of the kingdom of heaven: and whatsoever thou shalt bind on earth shall be bound in heaven: and whatsoever thou shalt loose on earth shall be loosed in heaven."

Then Jesus charged them that they should tell no man of Him. And He began to teach

them, that the Son of man must suffer many things, and be rejected of the elders, and of the chief

priests, and scribes, and be *killed* and after three days rise again.

Decius watched as Peter took Jesus aside and began to reproach Him.

But Jesus turned about and looked at His disciples before He rebuked Peter, saying, "Get

thee behind me. For thou savourest not the things that be of God, but the things that be of men."

On the six day journey to Jericho, Jesus summoned Peter and the sons of thunder, John

and James. They followed him up to a high mountain, leaving the rest of them to find food and

make a camp for the night. When the three returned, for Jesus had stayed alone on the mountain

to pray, Peter joined Andrew and Philip, as was his wont.

John and James sought out Decius and Matthew. John talked rapidly, while James kept an

embarrassed silence. "The Lord was transfigured before us. His face did shine as the sun, and His

raiment was white as the light. And Moses and Elias appeared and talked to Him."

James spoke, "Peter said unto Him, 'Jesus, Lord, it is good for us to be here; if thou wilt,

let us make here three tabernacles; one for Thee and one for Moses, and one for Elias.'"

John nodded excitedly. "While Peter spoke, behold a bright cloud overshadowed them;

and behold a voice out of the cloud, said, '*This is my beloved Son, in whom I am well pleased;*

hear ye him.'"

"We fell on our faces and were sore afraid." James nearly whispered in awe. "But Jesus

came and touched us, and said, 'Arise, and be not afraid.'"

Decius followed Matthew back to his sleeping pallet. Matthew brought out his tax-

collecting paraphernalia and recorded the words of the Boarnerges brothers. "Will others

believe?" Matthew asked.

"I wish Salome were here to hear and witness all that I have seen. I'm not sure even this will be able to convince another to believe in Jesus's promise. I think the Lord knows who will believe and who will find stumbling blocks to belief. Accepting Him as their Savior is like jumping off a cliff. Those who do not believe cannot yet know the sureness and relief that comes when our hearts are able to welcome Him, our minds are awash in His love, and our bodies feel glorified."

A smile radiated from Matthew. "I'll mark you down as a believer."

"Once and always," Decius said.

<u>Chapter Nine</u>

"But if ye had known what this meaneth, 'I will
have mercy, and not sacrifice,' ye would not have
condemned the guiltless. For the Son of man is Lord
even of the Sabbath day."

(Dan 7:13; Matt 12:7-8)

Jericho, 30 AD

The long boat trip down Palestine's waterways from Caesaer Philippi to the Jordan River,

down the Sea of Galilee to the river's southern outlet, and then on foot beside the Dead Sea to

Jericho gave Decius time to reflect on the consequences of Jesus's prophecy coming true. Was

this new rabbi much of a threat to the priests of Jerusalem? Would he be killed? His spiritual

kingdom couldn't hurt the Roman occupation. How could might fight against right thoughts?

Nevertheless, subservience was not part of Jesus's teachings. Would forgiveness and love

strengthen a man's soul beyond the point of submission? If Palestine attempted to remove

Rome's rule, where would Sextus, he and Salome flee? Would Rome welcome them as

Christians who attempted to fight against Rome? For Rome would prevail, Decius was certain.

Sextus must be wondering about the future, too.

Matthew sought Decius out. "Your brow is knitted into permanent worry. Marriage to

Salome cannot be troubling you."

"What think thee of the Lord's predictions?"

"Of the priests wanting to murder anyone who might threaten their monetary domain?"

"Is it only the money?" Decius searched out Judas Iscariot, who stood in his customary stance, hand on his hip purse.

"Power over the people, even for a priest, must be satisfying." Matthew shook his head. "At least Jesus teaches us to be humble before those we serve. Are you thinking of Rome hearing about our spiritual rebellion."

"Even the word frightens all of Rome." Decius touched his breast, where his heart raced. He had again traded his leather armor for the long white robe Mary provided each of them. She was a shrewd woman. With their dark beards and long hair flowing past their shoulders not many could distinguish one disciple from another…except that Jesus was as tall as Decius, whose blond hair marked him as Roman. "We must trust in God," Decius said, accepting his fate as one tied to his Savior's.

Matthew hung his head in prayer or resignation, too.

The eleven apostles followed Jesus down the road to Jericho. Decius stumbled on the path. He caught himself wondering if he was unprepared for marriage to Salome. His mind was cluttered with conflicting thoughts, happiness tried to inch out the troubling remembrance of Jesus foretelling His death. How would Salome be able to believe Jesus said he would rise from the grave? Should he not reveal his worries to his future wife? Should he fold Salome in his arms and let the destiny of the rabbi unfold as it was wont?

Jesus walked rapidly through old Jericho towards its suburb of Bethany. Decius wondered if Ide's parents would attend the wedding ceremony in Lazarus's house. Magdalen and Mary, no doubt, worked wonders for the wedding feast. But could Lazarus agree to wed a Jewish maiden to a Roman, even if Decius could claim Tetrarch Philip's consent and dowry? How much time would he be allowed to spend with Salome before they were wed? Should all his doubts be put aside to claim the maiden of his dreams, who he'd rescued and cloistered from the royal family for over a year?

As they approached the home of Lazarus, Peter was the one who linked arms with Decius. "Every bridegroom has doubts about his future," Peter said. "I was terrified of my mother-in-law. You can see the loving woman was no one to fear."

"But Herodias…," Decius realized there was plenty to fear from that hate-filled monster.

Peter scoffed. "Mary would never allow anyone to harm Salome or you."

Decius wasn't as certain of the powers of the mother of Jesus as Peter, but Mary had provided a safe haven for more than a year. "Here comes Thomas," Decius said.

Thomas ran first to Jesus, bowing to his rabbi in welcome. After Jesus passed by him, Thomas came to Decius. "Your bride is dressed for the wedding. Let's give you a quick bath and robe you for your future."

"Is she well?" Decius asked as he was hustled into the bathhouse.

Thomas called from the other side of the door. "Of course she's well. Every maiden is happy and healthy on her wedding day."

"I don't know the words for the ceremony." Decius protested, feeling a bit weak in the knees. Strengthening his tone, he asked, "Has Sextus Orlando arrived?"

"That Roman, Dorcas, and two hounds made Salome forget you were missing for an entire afternoon." Thomas laughed. "I'm afraid you are the man of the hour. I envy your love for each other."

Somehow, that settled Decius's stomach. He broadened his shoulders as if preparing for a war campaign and stepped out of the bathhouse. Thomas placed a dark robe of royal blue around his shoulders. Mary must have woven the magnificent cape for the occasion. Decius felt fine, anxious to see Salome's face.

*   *   *

Salome's silk veil, which Magdalen had salvaged from her hurried packing, covered her hair and half her face; but Salome could see Decius as he walked boldly towards her on the palm-strewn path to the wedding booth. Bells tied to the fringe of the tent made a bit of noise as Decius ducked his head to enter.

Lazarus called the gathered congregation to witness their rites. Decius took Salome's hand and filled her trembling palm with rings. She recognized five of her father's royal rings, then smiled up at her handsome man. Decius must have visited and convinced her father of his love. Salome chose the largest of the rings and placed the golden promise on Decius's finger.

Sextus leaned forward with a smaller gold ring for Salome. "Your mother's," he said to Decius.

Large tears escaped Decius's control and splashed onto their combined hands.

"Another blessing," Lazarus said for the newly married couple.

Home, the sheepdog, and Nether, the black hound, crowded into the wedding tent. They barked and jumped up excitedly next to Decius and Salome, as if they knew something joyful had occurred. Salome couldn't rebuke them, even though Rabbi Lazarus seemed shocked at the affront to the seriousness of their vows. "I feel like jumping up and down, too," she tried to explain.

Decius added, "We've waited for over a year."

"Not long in a long life of happiness before you," Lazarus said.

Jesus met them as they exited the tent. "Peace always," he said.

Mary, Martha, Magdalen, and Dorcas embraced Salome. Her own tears of happiness were running down Salome's face. She watched as the apostles congratulated her husband.

Bartholomew was uncharacteristically crying. "I'm so happy for you, Decius," he said between great sobs.

Peter led the disgraced fisherman away after speaking quietly to Decius. Salome heard Andrew and Philip give their congratulations in their most formal Greek language. Matthew continued an argument with Thomas before remembering his manners. He put his arm around Thomas and drew him towards Decius's chair.

Behind Decius, Sextus stood next to Judas Iscariot, not speaking but keeping a close watch. Salome noticed when Sextus leaned over Decius. She saw Decius hand over his stash of her father's dowry of rings to his long-time family friend. Salome also noted Judas Iscariot observed the transaction, too carefully.

Nathaniel, the man who was converted when Decius accepted Jesus's teaching, embraced Salome's tall Roman husband. She wished with all her heart she could claim she believed just to stop Decius's worry for her soul.

The younger apostles: Janus, Simon, and Jude crowded around Decius, sharing his limelight for a moment.

After nodding in Salome's direction, the mother of the sons of Zebedee spoke to Jesus, "Grant that these my two sons may sit, the one on Thy right hand, and the other on the left, in Thy kingdom."

The chattering wedding crowd grew silent. Jesus asked her slight-built sons, "Ye know not what ye ask. Are ye able to drink of the cup that I shall drink of, and to be baptized with the baptism that I am baptized with?"

John and James answered in unison, "We are able."

Jesus looked out across the crowd, above their heads, before He spoke. "...to sit on my right hand, and on my left, is not mine to give, but it shall be given to them for whom it is prepared of my Father."

When the remaining ten apostles heard His answer, they appeared moved with indignation against the two brethren. Salome watched as they turned their backs and busied themselves conversing with other wedding guests whom she did not recognize.

Magdalen and Mary stayed close to Salome, as if they were guarding her from any guests' censure. Sitting next to her husband at the main feast table, Salome heard Magdalen whisper to Mary. Salome perceived three words she hoped Decius had not heard, "...rebellion against Rome."

Dorcas was helping Lazarus's older sister, Martha, with the serving duties.

Finally, Martha approached Jesus, who was sitting next to Lazarus. "Lord, dost thou not care that my sister, Magdalen, hath left me to serve alone? Bid her therefore that she help me."

Jesus answered, "Martha, Martha, thou art careful and troubled about many things. But one thing is needful and Magdalen hath chosen that good part, which shall not be taken away from her."

Salome, frowning, tugged on Mary's sleeve wanting to understand His meaning. Mary whispered, "Magdalen believes in him."

Salome was suddenly saddened, as if Ide had died all over. Tears ran down her face. She felt grief-stricken on the happiest day of her life. Why couldn't she believe?

Decius noticed and enclosed her in his arms, "What is it, Salome?"

"I wish I could believe." Salome sobbed quietly trying to regain composure. "Why is it my soul will not take the teachings of Jesus in?"

Decius whispered close to her ear. "I think you will believe after all the resentments of evil done to you have been washed away."

*   *   *

When they were finally alone, Salome seemed too nervous to undertake any consummation of their wedding vows. She asked a thousand questions about her father, any miracles Jesus had performed in Casarea Philippi, their future in Nazareth, how many children he wanted and the wedding guests she hadn't known.

Decius decided the wedding night might be a long one. He answered every question but failed to mention how frail he thought her father, Philip, looked, or how Jesus had foretold His own death and resurrection, or that he had no idea what their future would include. He did describe one friend of Mary's, Joseph of Arimathea, as well as those surrounding Judas Iscariot: Rabbi Nicodemus, Zadoc the son of Hillel, and Kemayor, a Babylonian.

As he finished his long tale, Decius noticed Salome had fallen asleep in his arms. He didn't intend to shut his eyes. Decius re-filled the oil lamps. He feasted his eyes on his beloved, Salome, in all her young innocence and glory. He tasted her lips, smelled the scent of roses as he had when he'd first embraced her in Herod's palace at Machaerus. Decius touched the soft skin of her throat, buried his face into her soft curls, then gently untied the ribbons on her nightdress as she stirred and woke.

When the dawn arrived, Decius spoke to his redheaded bride, thankful for her affectionate lovemaking, "Domina."

The smile in Salome's green eyes reflected her happiness. "O optime Decius, fortissimos vir, Decius."

*   *   *

Salome hoped her matronly composure was obvious to Mary and Magdalen as she joined them in Martha's cooking room.

"The bride descends," Magdalen said, rushing to embrace her.

"Don't ask me any questions." Salome knew her tone implied justified pride in her husband.

"Then while we break our morning fast," Mary said, "Let me tell you a story about Jesus." Dorcas joined the other women at the table to listen while they ate. Mary said, "In the sixth month of the new year, the angel Gabriel was sent from God unto my city in Galilee, Nazareth." Mary seemed lost in a far-off land. A rapturous memory transfigured her face from within. "I conceived my firstborn."

"But how could that be," Martha asked, "if you were never with a man?"

"The power of the Highest overshadowed me." Mary continued her tale, "When Herod was King of Judae, a priest named Zacharias was married to my mother's sister. They were both daughters of Aaron. My mother, Ann, was older than Elizabeth. You know how Zacharias was struck dumb when he wouldn't believe that Elizabeth was with child. He did speak later to name their child, John. But you don't know when I was carrying my firstborn, beloved son, I visited my aunt. When she saw me, her child leapt in her womb. Elizabeth said to me, 'Through the tender mercy of our God, whereby the dayspring from on high both visited us.' And I answered as boldly." Mary's chin lifted. "'…to guide our feet into the way of peace.'"

"Elizabeth read to Zacharias when he was mute. They had grown old together and spent much time reading the law. While I was with child, not to give offense to my husband, I resided with my Aunt Elizabeth in the hill country in a small city of Judae. She taught me to read the prophets and we found many places describing both our sons' missions on earth. I brought Elizabeth the news of what happened when my son, Jesus, first visited her son, John the Baptist."

"John said to him, 'I need to be baptized of thee.'"

"But Jesus said, 'Suffer it to be so now for it becometh us to fulfill all righteousness.'"

"When Jesus was baptized He went up straightway out of the water and lo, the heavens were opened unto Him and He saw the Spirit of God descending like a dove and lighting upon him. And lo a voice from heaven, saying, 'This is my beloved Son, in whom I am well pleased.'"

Salome wondered if she was already with child, patting her flat stomach. What would another life beginning inside of her feel like? Suddenly hungry, she reached for another soft sweetbread.

Mary spoke as if she no longer sat among the women in Lazarus's home; as if eternity should hear her words. "Caesar Augustus needed taxes, and when Cyrenius was governor of Syria, I convinced my husband, Joseph, to leave Nazareth to take us up to Bethlehem to be counted. It was the Fifteenth year of Tiberius Caesar, when Pontius Pilate became governor of Judea; Herod was king and lived in Jerusalem. We first saw Bethlehem from a hill which was covered with Cypress trees and shade-providing fig trees. The setting sun gave all the buildings

an orange glow. The trip had been long. I sympathized with my older husband as well as the poor

donkey who was carrying the load of two, my unborn child and me."

"Bethlehem's streets were narrow with no place for trees or grass. Our donkey had to

push its way through the crowds and mangy dogs. The buildings were four stories high in places.

Housewives threw their rubbish into the street. The stone paths were raised so that thin rivers of

offal and unmentionable waste mingled with the remains of suppers and wash water. The stench

was worse than the salt pools around the Dead Sea."

"I was finally able to draw a clean breath of air when we reached the edge of town. I was

happy there were no rooms to be let in the town. The stone cave among the arches of the Roman

aqueducts offered a pleasant respite. I credit my husband, Joseph, for finding us the perfect place

to bed down among the sweet- smelling animals in a stable. To calm any fears my husband might

have, I told him, 'I'd rather give birth among these least of God's creatures than near the

unhealthy breed who smell up that city.'

"Then, I felt a sublime release. Jesus was born of me."

Magdalen twisted a lock of her long red hair near her ear. Martha's hands rested in her

lap. Dorcas tilted her head as she listened to Mary's story. Salome reached for another roll.

Mary continued, "Angels guided the shepherds to us and a star brought wise men from

distant lands to view the Savior of the world. The foreigners even visited King Herod to inquire

as to our whereabouts. When they saw our humble circumstances, they understood Herod would

fear my child born in poverty might overthrow his rich kingdom. An angel came to warn Joseph,

my husband, so we journeyed to Egypt to escape the slaughter of male children under the age of

two that Herod demanded. When Herod died, the angel returned to Joseph, and we re-settled in
Nazareth."

Salome acknowledged Mary, the mother of Jesus, was incapable of subterfuge. The story
was intriguing, believable. "I love you," she said to Mary.

"And I you," Mary said. "If you ever are in need, you have only to ask."

"Could you make me willing to believe in your son, Jesus?" Salome asked, close to tears
in her earnestness.

"We must let you speak to your mother, Herodias, to show her you've forgiven her
wickedness," Mary advised.

"Decius says the same," Salome said, almost convinced to summon the courage needed to
approach her insane mother.

*   *   *

Pool of Siloam, Nisan (March) 30 AD

The Nazarene, His family, apostles, and Decius's family set out from Jericho in the spring
month of Nisan for the second Passover in Jesus's public life. Dorcas stayed behind with Martha
to mind Lazarus's gardens and the dogs.

The Sabbath day was warm. Decius looked back at his smiling wife, who had her arms
linked with Mary and Magdalen. All was right with the world. But Decius went to alert Matthew
as they neared the holy city, when a group of Pharisees from the temple joined the ranks of
people gathering around Jesus.

"They mean to trap him to bring charges before the Chief Priests," Matthew
acknowledged the threat to Lazarus.

Sextus asked them, "Have you noticed the twelve of you have been outfitted by Mary to be indistinguishable from each other, except for the smaller sons of Zebedee?"

Matthew laughed, "You, Decius and Janus balance the group with your tallness."

"Which is mirrored in Jesus's height," Lazarus said.

The group was passing through a field of golden, fully tasseled winter wheat. Several of the apostles reached out their hands to taste the inviting, ripe kernels of wheat. But when the Pharisees saw it, they said unto Jesus, "Behold thy disciples do that which is not lawful to do upon the Sabbath day."

But He said unto them, "Have ye not read what David did, when he was an hungred, and they that were with him; How he entered into the house of God, and did eat the showbread, which was not lawful for him to eat, neither for them which were with him, but only for the priests? Or have ye not read in the law, how that on the Sabbath days the priests in the temple profane the Sabbath, and are blameless? But I say unto you, that in this place is one greater than the temple. But if ye had known what this meaneth, 'I will have mercy, and not sacrifice,' ye would not have condemned the guiltless. For the Son of man is Lord even of the Sabbath day."

Decius and Sextus positioned themselves closer to Jesus's side as he entered the southern Water Gate of Jerusalem. The Pharisees whispered together in apparent disagreement trailing behind the group. And there was a man nearby, who had his hand withered. And one of the Pharisees seeking to set a trap asked Jesus, "Is it lawful to heal on the Sabbath days?"

Jesus said, "What man among you, that shall have one sheep, and if it fall into a pit on the Sabbath day, will he not lay hold on it, and lift it out? How much then is a man better than a sheep? Wherefore it is lawful to do well on the Sabbath days." Then saith he to the man, "Stretch forth thy hand."

And the man stretched forth his hand and it was restored whole like as the other. Then the Pharisees held a council against him, how they might destroy him.

But Jesus knew it and he withdrew himself. Great multitudes followed him, and he healed them all and charged them that they should not make him known. Then they brought to him one possessed, blind and dumb: and Jesus healed him, insomuch that the blind and dumb both spoke and saw. And all the people were amazed.

But when the Pharisees heard about it, they said, "This fellow doth not cast out devils, but by Beelzebub the prince of the devils.

And Jesus again knew their thoughts and answered their accusations. "Every kingdom divided against itself is brought to desolation; and every city or house divided against itself shall not stand: And if Satan cast out Satan, he is divided against himself; how shall then his kingdom stand? …and he that is not with me is against me; and he that gathereth not with me scattereth abroad. …o generation of vipers, how can ye, being evil, speak good things? For out of the abundance of the heart the mouth speaketh."

Then a certain scribe following the Pharisees said, "Master, we would see a sign from thee."

Jesus answered, but Decius only heard the last few words, while he watched the scribe write them in Greek. "For as Jonas was three days and three nights in the whale's belly; so shall the Son of man be three days and three nights in the heart of the earth."

Salome touched Decius's arm. "Is He claiming He will come back from the dead?"

Decius drew her away. "What does Mary say is in His future?"

"We haven't read from the scrolls lately." She twisted in his arms to see if any one had heard, then whispered to him, "When we return to Nazareth, we'll be able to search out His future."

"Mary seems more worried than on our first trip." Decius wanted to continue to stay near Jesus, but husbanding a wife required him to see to her safety first. "The Pharisees might detain Jesus at any moment. Will you stay close to Mary and Magdalen while Sextus and I try to guard him?"

Salome's great green eyes widened in fear. Decius drew her veil more closely around her face, so that no one might recognize her by the beauty of her eyes, alone. "I'll do as you say, husband." Salome slowly walked away.

Decius felt bereft of the impetuous child as soon as she left his side. Salome had grown into a mature woman before his eyes.

As the group drew near the Pool of Siloam, a man blind since birth approached Jesus. And John asked him, saying, "Master, who did sin, this man, or his parents, that he was born blind?"

Jesus answered, "Neither that this man sinned, nor his parents: but that the works of God should be manifest in him. I must work the works of him that sent me, while it is day: the night cometh, when no man can work. As long as I am in the world, I am the light of the world."

When He had thus spoken, He spat on the ground, and made clay of the spittle, and He anointed the eyes of the blind man with the clay, and said unto him, "Go, wash in the pool of Siloam."

And they followed him as he went his way. Decius helped the blind man down the steps to the edge of the pool. The man washed and came back up the steps seeing. And the Pharisees questioned him closely. Decius overheard one of them say, "This man is not of God, because he keepeth not the Sabbath day."

Another argued, "How can a man that is a sinner do such miracles? Since the world began was it not heard that any man opened the eyes of one that was born blind."

The oldest of their group said, "If this man were not of God, he could do nothing."

Decius left them knowing there would be a continuing division among them, which might give Jesus time to continue his preaching ministry.

*   *   *

Herod's Palace, Jerusalem

Salome had returned to Mary's side, but she intended to face her fears with an act of courage. "Mother, will you go with me to see Herodias?"

Without any hesitation, Mary and Magdalen agreed to the adventure. They were soon battling the Passover crowds elbowing their way through the Essene Gate. The women exited the lower city into the Hinnom Valley south of the city. Then they rounded the eastern, lower half of Jerusalem and entered Gennath Gate to gain access to Herod's Palace in the Upper City.

Salome looked up at the Tower of Mariamne shining with the late afternoon sun. She remembered looking back at the structure and wondering where her mother was when she was dressed as a boy, escaping to Mary's sanctuary with Decius. Though only two years had passed, Salome thought of herself as twenty years older. "We can enter through the servants' door unobserved," Salome told her two companions.

No torches were lit in the staircase leading to the upper royal chambers. Salome never considered those serving her had spent their time burdened in these dark halls. "God forgive me," she prayed.

"That's a prayer that our Lord always hears," Mary said.

"Amen," Magdalen's voice was subdued in the gloom.

They reached an outer porch overlooking the courtyards of the Upper City. Across from them the older palace of Herod Antipas was shadowed, but the northern towers of Antonia's Fortress shone. The dome of the rock rose upward, pregnant with meaning.

Mary gasped and Magdalen went to her. "What is it, Mother?"

"I cannot tell," Mary said. "But I know no good is in the future for when next I see Jerusalem."

"Maybe the shadows of the staircases have left their mark." Salome tried to cheer her friends. "Come, I'll show you my rooms."

An ancient servant pulled at Salome's veil, then she dropped to one knee. "Princess!"

"Please, Lydia, tell no one you've seen me." Salome was heartened to find they were still alone in the passage to her room. "I want to speak to Herodias. Where will I find her?"

Lydia stroked Salome's face. "Child, you're a woman now. Your mother is in Rome. If she returns while I'm still alive, what message shall I give her?"

"Is my room safe to adjourn to?"

"Of course, Mistress. Shall I bring food?"

"No, Lydia. You might be in danger if it's known I visited. But come with me." Salome ushered Mary and Magdalen into her old suite of rooms. She busied herself finding a wax tablet and stylus to write Herodias a note.

Magdalen's curiosity caused her to push through racks of clothing. She peeked into several chests of jewelry on the marble tables. Mary stood quietly looking out the verandah. Magdalen opened a vial of perfume and brought it to Mary.

Mary shook her head. "It smells like myrrh."

"Are you going to take any of your possessions with you?" Magdalen asked.

"No," Salome said. "I'll just leave a note for Herodias. What shall I say, Mother."

Mary turned to her. "What have you written, so far?"

"Only that I am sorry if I worried her, that I'm fine...." Salome held the stylus ready for Mary's dictate.

"And that you forgive her with all your heart," Mary said.

"Is it all right to say I think of her with a spirit of forgiveness?" Salome wasn't ready to wipe away all the injury.

"That will have to do," Mary said. "We best leave."

Salome entrusted the tablet to Lydia. "Let her find it, where you won't be incriminated."

"I know just the place," Lydia said. "Her chariot driver has a room next to hers."

"Perfect," Salome was surprised to hear herself laugh. A burden had been lifted from her heart. "And Herod?" she asked.

Lydia shook her head. "We all think the Tetrarch is close to madness. Herod thinks the new rabbi from Nazareth, Jesus, is John the Baptist, risen from the dead. He's in constant pain when he eats."

Mary drew Salome towards the dark stairway and they left her old life behind.

Chapter Ten

"'For the people's heart is waxed gross, and their ears are dull of hearing, and their eyes they have closed; lest at any time they should see with their eyes and hear with their ears, and should understand with their heart, and should be converted, and I should heal them.'"

(Is 6:9-10; Matt 13:25)

Nazareth

On the way home to Nazareth, Salome welcomed the fact that Decius refused to leave her side. The crowds had not dissipated after they left Jerusalem. Usually the Passover pilgrims would adjourn to their various lives in the villages along the road, but the people were loathe to leave the peaceful environs surrounding Jesus.

Decius had enlightened her about the hatred Jesus encountered from the ruling priests in Jerusalem. Believing the holy men intended to kill one of their own, a gifted rabbi, seemed highly unlikely to Salome. "I worried when you and the other women left the group," Decius said.

"I was about my mother's business," Salome said. "You know, trying to forgive her."

"You went to the palace?" Decius grabbed her and embraced her as if she'd just returned from a perilous sea voyage. "How did she respond?"

"I walked out alive." Salome tried to push herself free of his arms. "Really, Decius, I shouldn't tease. She wasn't there, so Mary agreed I could leave her a written forgiveness."

After kissing her, Decius finally released her. "Please tell me when you plan to leave again."

Salome reached for his robe. "Wait. Herodias went to Rome. They say Herod is going mad." Salome stood close to Decius waiting and watching for his reaction. "Herod believes Jesus is John the Baptist come back to life."

"He is mad."

"But, husband," Salome pursued the subject. "Jesus believes He will return from the dead. I heard Him with my own ears."

Decius nodded. "I'm more worried about Jesus being harmed than His predictions for the future of our belief."

Salome had to admit Decius and the devoted audience staying with Jesus did act as if they might witness the sudden disappearance of their prophet.

Spring also held its breath as the month remained unseasonably cold. Salome looked in vain for any sign of sprouting wild flowers along their path home. An icy drizzle should have encouraged the multitude to find shelter.

On the third evening, Jesus's disciples said to Him, "This is an inhospitable place, and the time is now past; send the multitude away, that they may go into the villages, and buy themselves victuals."

Jesus was moved with compassion. "They need not depart," He said, "Give ye them to eat."

And Salome heard them tell Him, "We have here but five loaves, and two fishes."

Jesus said, "Bring them hither to me."

The clouds seemed chased away by His words. A flock of yellow finches brought the sun to rest at Jesus's feet. Salome knelt at the beauty suddenly surrounding them. Decius laid his heavy hand on her shoulder. She welcomed its anchoring effect on her emotions of rapture. A fresh breeze from an out-of-sight field of lavender perfumed the air. When Salome turned her face up to Decius, the heat of the revealed sun warmed her cheek.

Jesus commanded the multitude to sit down on the grass. He took the linen filled with the five loaves and two fishes and looking up to heaven; He blessed and broke them and gave the loaves to His disciples, who distributed them to the crowd of at least a thousand.

After they had eaten, the disciples gathered the fragments which filled twelve baskets.

Salome helped Mary and Magdalen to gather up the robes they had laid on the grass when they sat down to eat. Clouds were gathering, and a cold breeze threatened more rain. Decius helped Salome fold the blankets. "Are you now a believer?" His hand indicated the line of twelve baskets before each of the disciples.

Judas Iscariot headed the line of apostles. Salome could see the workings of his greedy mind as he assessed the value of the contributions. Peter was poking at the fish in a basket as if to determine their freshness. Bartholomew was happily shooing flies away from three baskets of broken bread sitting in front of Andrew, Philip and himself. Thomas gazed at the gathering clouds and draped his cloak over his basket of food gifts. Janus, Jude, and Simon were still sitting in a dazed state before overflowing remnants of the meal. John still held a basket, while his brother, James had covered one with a wicker lid to keep off the first sprinkles of rain. Matthew stood under a makeshift tent of his robe held by his friend, Nathaniel. Matthew was, no doubt, inscribing the recent feeding of the multitude into his journal.

Salome thought to answer her husband with a lie about her belief, but the memory of her father's teachings held sway. "Lies only grow, when spoken."

"What lie?" Decius asked, almost harshly.

"I want to tell you I believe and that's only what you want to hear from me, but those words would be a lie." Salome wished for a moment she didn't love her husband so much.

Decius ran his giant hands through his blond hair. "But look at all the food."

"We carried enough for you," Salome said. "The crowd knows the journey home is often long."

"You're saying no miracle occurred!" Decius's pale complexion turned a beet color. "But you knelt when Jesus blessed the bread."

"Don't you remember the beauty of the moment?" Salome hung her head. "For you I know there was a great miracle. You believe Jesus conjured up this bounty." Decius turned his back and shambled away. Salome turned to Mary. "Mother, what do you believe?"

"I believe my son has His heavenly Father's blessing on the food provided." Mary smiled and embraced Salome.

Salome nestled close to the woman who loved her more than her birth mother was capable of doing. "Will I ever believe?"

Mary disengaged herself from Salome, but held tightly to her shoulders. "You, Salome, will be one of His most devoted followers, someday. All your children will find you blessed with belief."

*   *   *

Capernaum, Tishri (Sep) 30 AD

There would be no harvest this year in Palestine. The rainy spring was followed by winds and unseasonable ice storms into the heart of summer. Then the rains continued, washing out the fields and leaving plants yellowed and withered. Decius and Sextus argued about the number of storehouses of grain needed to see Decius's adopted country through the winter's coming famine.

Jewish traditional harvest booths did appear in the farmers' empty fields, but the harsh realities couldn't be swept away with piety. The remembrance of the tribe's trials when they left Egypt did sustain their belief as God's chosen ones.

Incredibly, Decius had hung onto his faith through the long summer. He had hardly begun to feel pride in Salome's bulging waistline and slight stomach. Salome had let him feel the movement of life before it was too late. Mary said Salome's time was not fulfilled because the baby came too soon to live for long. Sextus assured him other children would follow. The wrenching ordeal of watching Salome grieve over their stillborn child, a boy, went on and on. Decius prayed daily, "Help me to trust you more, Lord."

Salome avoided his touch. Her green eyes lost their luster; she walked slowly contemplating the ground. Her smile, all the sun Decius needed for any day, was seldom seen. Her dogs were as depressed as she. Home's age wore on him, and his health seemed to fail completely when Salome was unable to keep her spirits up. After his death, Nether refused to eat and died less than a month after his friend.

Mary insisted Salome needed a trip to revive her spirits. Sextus agreed so Decius brought her to Capernaum to seek out the peace surrounding Jesus.

At the first meal in the dining hall of Peter's compound, Jesus spoke to his apostles. "Go not unto the way of the Gentiles, and into any city of the Samaritans enter ye not: But go rather to the lost sheep of the house of Israel. Preach that the kingdom of heaven is at hand. Heal the sick, cleanse the lepers, raise the dead, cast out devils: freely ye have received, freely give. Provide neither gold, nor silver, nor brass in your purses, Nor scrip for your journey, neither two coats, neither shoes, nor yet staves: for the workman is worthy of his meat. And into whatsoever city or town ye shall enter, enquire who in it is worthy, and there abide till ye go thence. And if the house be worthy, let your peace come upon it: but if it be not worthy, let your peace return to you. Behold, I send you forth as sheep in the midst of wolves: be ye therefore wise as serpents, and harmless as doves. But beware of men: for they will deliver you up to the councils, and they will scourge you in their synagogues. Take no thought how or what ye shall speak: for it shall be given you in that same hour what ye shall speak. The Spirit of your Father shall speak in you. He that receiveth you receiveth me, and he that receiveth me receiveth him that sent me.

Then he began to upbraid the cities wherein most of his mighty works were done, because they repented not. "And thou Capernaum, which art exalted unto heaven, shall be brought down to hell: for if the mighty works, which have been done in thee, had been done in Sodom, it would have remained until this day."

Decius was surprised when Peter didn't argue with his rabbi; for there they were the twelve and Peter's family and friends, all believing. Except for Salome. Decius left the dining hall in search of his wife. He found her in the cooking hut with Peter's mother-in-law. The steam and warmth of the room rose up to greet him. Salome stayed seated near the fire, peeling carrots for their next meal. Decius pulled a chair next to hers. He leaned his head on her dear shoulder, smelled roses, which seemed to emanate from her skin. He reached one hand under her headscarf and touched her soft hair. "Salome," he said, wishing he could demand her to return to her youthful gaiety.

Thomas had followed him into the cooking shed. "Ask her," Thomas said. "I want to hear why she thinks Jesus condemns all of Capernaum."

Salome lifted her head. She looked first at Decius then answered Thomas. "I understand. If Jesus feels He cannot avoid death at the hands of His own priests, why would He not condemn all of the living, who will go on after He is dead? Have you noticed how He has killed the fields, the seasons, the flowers, the harvest, my dogs…my child?"

Decius's heart broke. "Come away, Thomas," he said. "My wife is till grieving for our child."

"Pray for us, Salome," Thomas said. "We all need your love to return."

Decius was suddenly angered. He pushed Thomas outside. "Did you say Salome loves you?"

"Her affection for the universe spreads out before us all," Thomas said in his defense. "When will she be restored?"

Decius began to weep. His anger seeped out of him as he was overwhelmed by the loss of his wife's happiness. "I pray every day to see her joy return."

Thomas and Decius returned to listen to their rabbi. Judas Iscariot was standing near the doorway and Jesus turned at the noise of their entrance.

Jesus said, "I thank thee, O Father, Lord of heaven and earth, because thou has hid these things from the wise and prudent." Then Jesus turned his back on them and continued, "and has revealed them unto babes."

Decius remembered Judas's collection of coins he had hidden under the flagstones behind the dining hall. Should he warn Thomas of Judas's avariciousness? But the peace accompanying the Lord's voice flooded over him.

"Even so, Father: for so it seemed good in thy sight. All things are delivered unto me of my Father; and no man knoweth the Son, but the Father; neither knoweth any man the Father, save the Son, and he to whomsoever the Son will reveal him. Come unto me, all ye that labour and are heavy laden, and I will give you rest. Take my yoke upon you, and learn of me, for I am meek and lowly in heart; and ye shall find rest unto your souls. For my yoke is easy, and my burden is light."

Decius prayed for his wife, for all of Israel, for himself, and for his rabbi's safety. When he was finished, he noticed he was alone in the dining hall.

Peter stood outside the door. "Come with us fishing," Peter said. "Salome needs a quiet time to be restored."

"Mary and Sextus told me to take her on this trip to cheer her." Decius was at a loss, Salome's mood had not improved. "I'll bring her with us."

*   *   *

Sea of Galilee

Salome welcomed Decius's invitation to join the apostles and Jesus on their fishing trip. In the company of other women, she couldn't shake off her feelings of failure. What had she done to cause the child to arrive too early? She spent hours ruminating going over every action, every particle of food she had eaten, love-making with Decius, even laughing too hard, but nothing explained the child's escape from her womb. As she stepped aboard Peter's boat, her spirits lifted. The boat rocked with the arrival of each apostle, making her giggle for the first time in months. Decius noticed and almost squashed her lightened frame of mind by his look of relief. But Salome refused to remember her sorrow, reaching out for his hand. "Husband," she said.

Trying not to let the others show his distress, Decius kissed her hand. A tear had escaped his bowed head, and Salome remembered his tears blessing her wedding ring. "You're back," he said, sitting next to her.

Salome moved closer to his shoulder, which trembled at her touch. They had not been intimate for a long time. "When next we are alone," she promised.

"Thomas," Decius called to his friend, "Come sit with us."

Thomas looked their way, then seemed to grow as he became aware of their altered state. "Peter," he cried, as if he wanted to draw the group's attention to them; but seemed to change his mind in mid-sentence. "This will be a great catch!"

Decius laughed.

Salome realized how selfish her suffering had made her. She'd dampened the life force of those around her. She sought out where Jesus was sitting in the boat. His head was bowed, unmindful of the shift in her universe. Her heart went out to Him. He was suffering for all their sins every day. She prayed for His safety, then realized Decius and the other disciples were probably doing the same.

Judas's back was to her as he sat in the stern, looking back toward Capernaum, the town Jesus had called home, but now had cursed because of the non-believers. Salome avoided looking into the state of her soul. The gladness she felt was sustaining her faith in her father's beliefs. She was happy her father, Philip, didn't know he'd lost a grandson. She shook her head, dismissing bad thoughts and endeavored to concentrate on the rest of the Apostles. Salome briefly glanced in Judas's direction, wondering if he'd brought along the coins Decius saw him bury behind Peter's house in Capernaum.

Wondering why the Lord trusted Judas, she asked Decius, "Is Judas Iscariot one of John-the-Baptist's early followers?"

"No," Decius said. "I don't remember him at Machaerus, when all his disciples listened to the prophet near his cell."

The young men: Janus, as curly haired as her blond husband, was elbowing Jude away from the side of the boat. Simon turned away from them disgusted at their childish wrestling. He caught Salome looking his way and blushed.

Decius nudged Salome. "Don't taunt the boys with your beauty."

Salome's anger reared its head, but she quickly turned away from the emotion, deciding instead to accept her husband's comment as a compliment instead of censure. "Thank you," she said. Her smile seemed to burn a permanent smile into his eyes.

Matthew sat scribbling as was his habit, while Andrew and Philip drew in a fine catch of fish. On the other side of the boat, Bartholomew was helping the brothers, John and James, to bring aboard a similar haul.

When they returned to shore, Salome made sure she thanked each of the apostles for allowing her to fish with them. Jesus did not return her smile, but He held her hand with both of His. Salome understood the kind gesture must have cost Him some expense of soul, as the slightest effort caused her when she was grieving. And here He was, knowing death was lurking close behind Him, yet He was able to offer silent comfort.

"I want to go home to Nazareth," Salome told Decius. "Mary might need me."

She saw Jesus raise His head at the mention of Mary's name, but He didn't look her way.

*   *   *

Nazareth, Tebeth (Dec) 30 AD

Decius knew he was neglecting his duties, but Sextus didn't rebuke him. Since Salome had lost their baby but regained her good spirits, Decius couldn't leave her side for more than a minute or two.

Their home in Nazareth stood next to the sentry station. Dorcas kept house for them when she wasn't attending to her own home with Sextus. Salome spent most of her time at Mary's or in the synagogue. With provisions in the town running low, Sextus and Decius were scheduled to hand out supplements from the city's grain storehouses, but Decius left the chore to Sextus's capable hands. Decius was happiest helping Salome, or waiting for Salome, or listening to Salome, or touching his sweet wife. The smell of roses guided his actions and Salome's scent was of this fresh flower.

Mary, the mother of Jesus, seemed to be aging quickly. Decius noticed each expedition up the hill to the Nazareth synagogue added a year to her face. He cautioned Salome one night, "Perhaps the trip up the hill is too much for Mary's age."

"The words of the Torah age Mary," Salome said. "Today we read in Isaiah, 'For they shall be ashamed of the oaks which ye have desired, and ye shall be confounded for the gardens that ye have chosen…For ye shall be as an oak whose leaf fadeth, and as a garden that hath no water.'"

"The famine will be relieved next year." Decius said.

"Mary's not concerned with the flowers in her window boxes not growing, or even for the lack of food." Salome spread her hands across their clean wooden table. "Mary's reading about the destruction of Israel, as if Jesus's words of condemnation were already written. In Isaiah it says, 'For behold, the Lord, the Lord of hosts, doth take away from Jerusalem and from Judah the stay and the staff, the whole stay of bread, and the whole stay of water. For Jerusalem is ruined and Judah is fallen: because their tongue and their doings are against the Lord, to provoke the eyes of His glory.'"

"Mary believes the famine will continue?" Decius asked.

Salome nodded her concern for Mary. "It is as if my grief for our son has transferred to Mary's heart."

Decius was silent. He remembered Jesus's dire words. "Does Mary know the priests are against her son?"

"Mary believes He will die." Salome's green eyes watered in sympathy.

Decius knelt at her side, enclosing Salome in his arms, more to comfort himself than her. "What can we do?"

"Stay with her," Salome said. "Today we read, 'And I will lay Israel waste: it shall not be pruned, nor digged; but there shall come up briers and thorns; I will command the clouds that they rain no rain upon it.'"

Decius was worried now. If rain was withheld next spring, the crops would fail for a second year.

Salome ran her fingers through her beautiful hair. "Mary does find Jesus's mission in most of the works of Isaiah. 'Therefore the Lord himself shall give you a sign; Behold, a virgin shall conceive, and bear a son and shall call his name Immanuel. For unto us a child is born, unto us a son is given: and the government shall be upon his shoulder: and his name shall be called Wonderful, Counselor, The mighty God, The everlasting Father, The Prince of Peace.'"

Decius hoped peace would remain in place in Israel. Times of famine were often times of unrest, according to Sextus. "Are you able to cheer Mary?"

"Her soul is very giving. Even in her worries she tends to me." Salome stood and led Decius to their bedroom. As she undressed before him, she continued to talk. "Mary told me she doesn't worry; she only prays without ceasing."

"As should we all," Decius said thankful to his very bones that his wife had returned to his ready arms.

Before they turned to sleep, Salome said, "The last verse we read before we left the synagogue today stays with me. 'Fear not, daughters of Sion; behold, thy King cometh, sitting on an ass's colt.'"

Chapter Eleven

"Tell ye the daughter of Sion, 'behold, thy King
cometh unto thee, meek, and sitting upon an ass,
and a colt the foal of an ass.'"

(2 Kin. 9:13; Matt 21:5)

Bethany, Nisan (Mar) 31 AD

Jesus, the apostles and his family had barely reached the town's outskirts when Salome

saw dust rising on the road from Jericho.

"It's Sextus's chariot," Decius said. After the two Romans had greeted each other with

great thumps on each others' backs, Decius returned to the group of women. "I must leave to

rejoin the troops in Jerusalem."

"Do they expect a rebellion?" Mary asked.

Decius dropped his head, then lifted his eyes to meet Mary's. "Sextus and I are

determined to save your son."

Mary reached for Decius's hand. "The Lord's will be done."

Salome had little time to process what was happening. "When will I see you?"

Decius stood at attention, already gone from the realm of women. "Never doubt my love."

And he left with Sextus in the chariot headed for Jerusalem.

Mary's embrace helped, but Salome somehow knew her universe, her marriage to the man she loved, the next breaths she let into her body would change her world forever. She placed one foot in front of the other on the road to Lazarus's home in Bethany, where she had married Decius a year ago.

*   *   *

Decius strapped on his leather breast armor, after stuffing the robe Mary had woven for him among Sextus's belongings. "How bad is the news?"

"Rufus tells me that Caiaphas, their high priest, has filed charges of blasphemy against Jesus. They mean to see Him killed, when He returns for Passover."

"Stop the chariot." Decius felt too weak to stand in the jostling chariot.

Sextus helped him to the side of the road, where a low wall served as their bench. "When Jesus walked in the temple in Solomon's porch for the winter feast of the tabernacle, the Jews baited Him." Decius hoped against hope that something could change the religious leaders' minds. Sextus shook his head in despair. "They asked Him, 'How long dost thou make us to doubt? If thou be the Christ, tell us plainly.'"

"Jesus answered them, 'I told you, and ye believed not: the works that I do in my Father's name, they bear witness of me. But ye believe not, because ye are not of my sheep, as I said unto you. My sheep hear my voice, and I know them, and they follow me: And I give unto them eternal life; and they shall never perish, neither shall any man pluck them out of my hand. My Father, which gave them me, is greater than all; and no man is able to pluck them out of my Father's hand. I and my Father are one.'"

Sextus shoulders slumped. "I was there. I saw them take up stones to stone Him. Jesus was unafraid and answered them, 'Many good works have I shewed you from my Father; for which of those works do ye stone me?'"

"They answered Him saying, 'For a good work we stone thee not; but for blasphemy; and because that thou, being a man, makest thyself God.'"

"Didn't Jesus explain to them?" Decius feared the worst. Sextus's face was ashen. Decius tried to remember the age of his friend but lost track of his thoughts when Sextus continued.

"Jesus argued with them. 'Is it not written in your law, I said, Ye are Gods? If he called them gods, unto whom the word of God came, and the scripture cannot be broken; Say ye of him, whom the Father hath sanctified, and sent unto the world, Thou blasphemest, because I said, I am the Son of God? If I do not the works of my Father, believe me not. But if I do, though ye believe not me, believe the works: that ye may know, and believe, that the Father is in me, and I in him.'"

"Did they try to detain Him?"

Sextus nodded. "He escaped but they're waiting for His return. I've convinced Rufus that you and I will wait for Jesus's arrival. Rufus doesn't need to know we mean to hide Him from the Romans, too. But we must find a way to save Him from the high priests without causing an outright rebellion."

"Where can we take Him?" Decius asked. "He's determined to win over His people."

*   *   *

Bethany, Nisan (Mar) 31 AD

Two days away from Lazarus's home, Magdalen and Martha approached the group of pilgrims that included Salome.

Martha said to Jesus, "Lord, behold, he whom thou lovest is sick."

Jesus heard and said, "This sickness is not unto death, but for the glory of God, that the Son of God might be glorified thereby." And He directed the disciples that they precede to Jerusalem for the Passover.

But his disciples tried to stop Him, knowing His peril. "Master, the Jews of late sought to stone thee; and goest though thither again?"

Jesus answered, "Are there not twelve hours in the day? If any man walk in the day, he stumbleth not, because he seeth the light of this world. But if a man walk in the night, he stumbleth, because there is no light in him." Then He added, " Our friend Lazarus sleepeth; but I go, that I may awake him out of sleep."

Peter said to Him, "Lord, if he sleep, he shall be well."

Salome worried that the Lord meant more than sleep and she heard Him tell them plainly.

"Lazarus is dead. And I am glad for your sakes that I was not there, to the intent ye may believe; nevertheless let us go unto him."

Thomas said to the group, "Let us also go, that we may die with Him."

Salome motioned for Thomas to join her. "Won't Decius be able to save Jesus from the high priests?"

"The people have been ruled too long by these law makers." Thomas pulled at his dark beard as if making it longer would improve his wisdom. "Stay with Mary at Lazarus's home. Don't come to Jerusalem for Passover."

Now Bethany was close to Jerusalem about fifteen furlongs off, so many Jews came to Martha and Magdalen to comfort them as they grieved for their brother, Lazarus. Salome could see Martha on the porch outside their home, when she first caught sight of Jesus approaching. She ran to meet Him, but Magdalen stayed inside.

Martha said to Jesus, "Lord, if thou hadst been here, my brother had not died. But I know, that even now, whatsoever thou wilt ask of God, God will give it thee."

Jesus said unto her, "Thy brother shall rise again."

Martha said, "I know that he shall rise again in the resurrection at the last day.

Jesus said, "I am the resurrection, and the life: he that believeth in me, though he were dead, yet shall he live: And whosoever liveth and believeth in me shall never die. Believest thou this?

She said to him, "Yea, Lord: I believe that thou art the Christ, the Son of God, which should come into the world."

And when she had said this, Salome followed her to call Magdalen. Salome was shocked at her friend Magdalen's condition. In her grief, Magdalen had torn out entire tufts of her beautiful red hair from her scalp. Her clothes were torn and flaked with ashes.

"The Master is come," Martha said, "and calleth for thee."

Mary and Martha helped to dress and veil Magdalen to meet the Lord. The Jews who were in the house to comfort them followed Magdalen.

Magdalen fell down at Jesus's feet, saying, "Lord, if thou hadst been here, my brother would not have died."

When Jesus saw Magdalen's tears and that the Jews who came with her were also weeping, he groaned in the spirit, and was troubled. And said, "Where have ye laid him?"

They told the Lord to follow them.

Jesus wept.

Salome heard the Jews acknowledge his grief. "Behold how He loved him!"

But others said, "Could not this man, which opened the eyes of the blind, have caused that even this man should not have died?"

When they arrived at the grave that had a stone laid at the entrance, Jesus said, "Take ye away the stone."

Martha intervened. "Lord, by this time he stinketh; for he hath been dead four days."

Jesus said, "Said I not unto thee, that, if thou wouldest believe, thou shouldest see the glory of God?"

And they rolled the stone aside; and Jesus lifted up his eyes and said, "Father, I thank thee that thou hast heard me. And I knew that thou hearest me always; but because of the people which stand by I said it, that they may believe that thou has sent me."

And he cried with a loud voice, "Lazarus, come forth."

Salome witnessed as the man, said to be dead, walked out of the grave, bound hand-and-foot with grave clothes, as was his face.

Jesus said, "Loose him, and let him go."

Many of the Jews present believed; but Salome knew some of them would report the staggering miracle to the Pharisees. Everyone else rejoiced around the risen Lazarus. Salome withdrew and in a private room mourned again for her dead son, still entombed in his small casket. She took off her head covering and combed out her long red curls, wondering if she should snatch her curls out by their roots. Would the Lord then would restore her son? Could Ide come back to life? Would she ever be able to hear her own baby cry? Would the dogs be too humble for Jesus to restore to life? Why Lazarus? True he was a beloved friend of the Lord's, a

high-ranking rabbi, who after all had sanctioned her marriage to Decius. Nevertheless, Salome

decided to let her hair show her rebellion against the injustice of death. She had forgiven her

mother's hatred, but now she found herself angry with God!

Mary noticed and nodded, as if in understanding or in sympathy for the losses the Lord

had not replaced for Salome.

*   *   *

Jerusalem

Decius and Sextus were present when the news of Lazarus's resurrection arrived in the

courts of the High Priest, where the Pharisees had gathered in council. They argued well into the

evening in a secret meeting. The heavy tapestries draped between the columns surrounding the

hall afforded the two Romans full access to their machinations. "What shall we do?" the

Pharisees asked each other.

"This man does many miracles." Joseph of Arimathea was present in the meeting. "My

friend Lazarus now walks after being in his tomb for four days."

Decius clapped his hand over his mouth. Salome was at Lazarus's house. Perhaps his

wife had been converted. Sextus touched Decius's shoulder, whispering, "Joseph has a house in

the lower city. We should approach him to let the apostles gather there."

In the council, Pharisees were encouraging the priests' outrage. "If we let Him alone, all

men will believe on Him; and the Romans shall come and take away our place and nation."

Caiaphas, the high priest that year said, "Ye know nothing at all, nor consider that it is

expedient for us, that one man should die for the people, that the whole nation perish not."

Joseph of Arimathea said, "Perhaps He won't come for Passover."

And the High Priest said that if any man knew where He was, he should show it, that they might take Him.

*   *   *

Palm Sunday

With her red hair flowing down her back, Salome followed the crowd as Jesus was welcomed into Jerusalem. Martha stayed behind to nurse Lazarus, but Mary and Magdalen attended the ceremony. Both were veiled, but neither censured Salome.

Some of the multitude spread their garments along the path they took through the city; others cut down branches from the trees and strew them along the way. The crowds cheered, "Hosanna to the son of David: Blessed is he that cometh in the name of the Lord, Hosanna in the highest."

Salome stayed close to Mary and the other women, but she searched the surrounding porches and outer courts of the temple for a glimpse of Decius. Tall Sextus in full Roman regalia approached her in the pressing crowds. As she tilted her head to question him, Sextus pointed to a battlement on the city wall behind her. Decius waved, but the crush of the crowd propelled Salome forward. She knew the priests and the Romans were on high alert. Crowds proclaiming the prophet's glory would not serve Him well. Rulers were not fond of those popular with the multitudes, especially those that rallied people in the streets.

Sextus had followed her through the crowd, touching her hair to get her attention. "Stay a minute." Salome could see Sextus was deeply disturbed and assumed he feared someone might recognize her royal lineage by the state of her hair. Instead, Sextus moved closer, lifting her hair to whisper directly into her ear. "Inform Mary, Joseph of Arimathea will provide the only safe

house in all of Jerusalem for the disciples and Jesus. Decius and I will meet you there, too."

Chapter Twelve

"And whosoever shall fall on this stone shall be
broken: but on whomsoever it shall fall, it will grind
him to powder."

(Is 8:14-15; Matt 21:44)

Joseph of Arimathea's House

Salome worried about the nearness of the Chief Priest's house in the Essene district of

Jerusalem; but perhaps Sextus was right, no one would expect Jesus to sup in the vicinity of the

man who possessed the power of life or death over Him. Mary was easily convinced Sextus had

chosen wisely. Joseph of Arimathea was a close ally of Mary's, counseling her when she was

troubled about her son's mission. Peter and Thomas on the other hand, clearly were troubled by

the Lord's decision to accept Joseph's hospitality.

When Decius and Sextus arrived, Mary directed the servants to set two more places at the

Lord's supper, but the Romans refused. Decius touched Salome's hair, before explaining, "We

must guard the entrances in case someone informs the priests where Jesus has taken refuge."

Salome attempted to explain her choice to be seen unveiled in public. "I want God to

know that I'm not reconciled to the loss we have endured."

Decius's stricken face reminded Salome how much Decius suffered from the loss of their firstborn son, too. "I am surprised how I still love the Lord," Decius said. "But when I think of being without His comfort, my heart faints within me." Decius drew Salome away from the others. "I thought Lazarus's resurrection would finally convince you of Jesus's divinity."

Salome tilted her head and twisted a curl close to her ear. "I was choked with anger when I saw Lazarus walk out alive from his grave. I admit it is possible a miracle happened. I'm not sure. Could Lazarus have been sleeping, as Jesus first told the apostles? Did his sisters mistakenly think he was dead? I have forgiven Herodias. Why, then, won't my soul accept the Lord's grace?"

Decius enclosed her in his arms. "Never doubt my love for you. Your integrity and honesty must be precious to the Lord, too." Then Decius smiled. "I remember something that might finally convince you. I heard Jesus tell Nicodemus, 'If I have told you earthly things, and ye believe not, how shall ye believe, if I tell you of heavenly things? For God so loved the world that he gave his only begotten Son, that whosoever believeth in him should not perish, but have everlasting life."

Salome was called back to the women, to help serve the Lord's Supper; but she kept the thought about God giving His only son for their redemption close to her heart. If Jesus was destined to die, He would return to his Father in Heaven. But her son was gone from her world. Perhaps she would need to wait until she met death to know her own son. Salome grieved because they hadn't thought of a name for the child, who arrived into the world not alive. She was comforted nevertheless, when the Lord accepted a piece of unleavened bread from her hands. Decius was right, the Lord knew her heart, and yet He still loved her.

Joseph of Arimathea visited with Mary at the table in his kitchen where the women were eating. "The threat is real."

"I trust the Lord on high knows what is likely to happen."

"Can't you talk to Him?" Salome asked on the way through the room to take more wine to Joseph's guests. "He could leave Palestine, go west among the mountains where John the Baptist stayed."

"My son knows his destiny." Mary stopped eating. "I feel heart-broken, but how can I explain.... I ask the Lord to help me trust."

Salome returned to the dining hall. Jesus sat in the middle of the table facing the kitchen door. He strained to see past her. So, Salome propped the door open, in order for Him to see Mary, and she Him.

Peter and Philip sat on His right hand and the brothers, John and James, were at His left. At the head of the table Judas Iscariot was flanked by Matthew on one side and Thomas on the other. Andrew was seated at the foot of the table with Bartholomew and Simon. Jude and Janus helped bring in the large platters of bitter herbs, fruits, and vegetables being served with the Passover lamb. Salome thought they needed more candles to light the repast, but Joseph said it would be inappropriate.

The solemn meal began.

Peter started the opening prayer, and the guests joined in "Blessed art Thou, O Eternal, our God, King of the Universe, Creator of the fruit of the vine."

And John continued, "Blessed art thou, O Eternal, our God, King of the Universe, who selected us from among all people and exalted us among nations, and did sanctify us with His commandments. And thou, O Eternal, our God, has given us festival days for joy, this feast of the unleavened bread, the time of our deliverance in remembrance of the departure from Egypt. For us hast Thou selected, and sanctified from among all nations, in that Thou caused us to inherit Thy holy festival days. Blessed art Thou, O Eternal, who hallowest the Sabbath and Israel and the festival days."

Matthew prayed, "Blessed art Thou, O Eternal, our God, King of the Universe, who has preserved us alive; sustained us, and brought us to this season."

The guests washed their hands.

Peter dipped a small piece of parsley into saltwater and distributed it to all. The group responded with "Blessed art Thou, O Eternal, our God, King of the Universe Creator of the fruits of the earth."

Then Peter took the middle piece of bread and broke it in two. He left one half between two whole sections and wrapped the larger half in a cloth. He set it aside, then prayed again, "Because we were slaves unto Pharaoh in Egypt, and the Eternal, our God, brought us forth thence with a mighty hand and an outstretched arm. And if the Most Holy, blessed be He, had not brought forth our ancestors from Egypt, we and our children and our children's children would still be in bondage to the Pharaohs in Egypt. Therefore, even if we were all of us wise, all of us men of knowledge and understanding, all of us learned in the Law, it nevertheless would be incumbent upon us to speak of the departure from Egypt; and all those who speak of the departure from Egypt, are accounted praiseworthy."

Jesus stood. "Verily I say unto you, that one of you shall betray me."

The apostles gasped in unison, then every one of them said in his turn, "Lord, is it I?"

And Jesus sat down, but said. "The Son of man goeth as it is written of Him: but woe unto that man by whom the Son of man is betrayed! It had been good for that man if he had not been born."

Then Judas Iscariot answered, "Master is it I?"

Jesus said unto him, "Thou hast said."

Judas covered his head with his red cloak and left the chamber, brushing past Sextus who was stationed at the back door. Salome watched as Sextus alerted Decius, and they followed Judas toward the High Priest's house.

Andrew rose from the foot of the table and asked Jude and Janus, the youngest members of the disciples to sit down with them, then he asked Jude, "Why is this night different than all other nights?"

Jude answered, "Because we eat the unleavened bread and bitter herbs."

Peter stood and asked, Janus, "Why do we open doors?"

"To let in the prophet, Elijah," Janus said.

Jesus lifted his cup to salute His mother.

Peter prayed again, "And it is that promise which has been the support of our ancestors and of ourselves, for not only one has risen up against us, but in every generation some have arisen against us to annihilate us, but the Most Holy, blessed be He, always delivered us out of their hands."

The guests said together, "How many abundant favors hath the Omnipresent performed upon us."

John stood on his tiptoes and asked young Simon, "Why do we eat bitter herbs this night rather than any other night?'

"It reminds us of the bitter and cruel way the Pharaoh treated the Jewish people," Simon answered, "when they were slaves in Egypt."

Jesus took the unleavened bread and blessed it and broke it into pieces and gave it to the disciples, saying, "Take eat; this is my body, which is given for you. Do this for the remembrance of me."

After supper Jesus took the cup of wine, and when He had given thanks, He gave it to them, saying, "Drink ye all of you: For this is my blood of the new testament, which is shed for many for the remission of sins. Whenever you drink it, do this for the remembrance of me. And I say unto you, I will not drink henceforth of this fruit of the vine, until that day when I drink it new with you in my Father's kingdom."

Then Peter led them in a Passover hymn, "For all those things, O Eternal, our God, will we give thanks unto Thee, and praise Thee. Blessed be Thy name continually, in the mouth of every living creature, for ever and ever; as it is written: 'When thou hast eaten, and art satisfied, then shalt thou bless the Eternal, Thy God for the good land which He hath given thee.' Blessed art Thou, O Eternal, for the gift of the land, and for the food."

And they prayed in unison, "Praise the Eternal, all ye nations; praise Him, all ye people; for His mercy prevaileth over us, and the truth of the Eternal endureth forever. Hallelujah!"

After some discussion, the apostles and Jesus agreed that it would be safe to walk in the gardens of the Mount of Olives.

Salome followed close behind them into Gethsemane.

*   *   *

Gethsemane

Salome stayed in the shadows under the gnarled olive trees away from the main path through the gardens. The Lord's clear words carried in the cool spring evening.

Then Jesus said to them, "All ye shall be offended because of me this night: for it is written, 'I will smite the shephered, and the sheep of the flock shall be scattered abroad.' But after I am risen again, I will go before you into Galilee."

Peter answered, "Though all men shall be offended because of Thee, yet will I never be offended."

Jesus said, "Verily I say unto thee, that this night, before the cock crow, thou shalt deny me thrice."

Peter said, "Though I should die with Thee, yet will I not deny Thee."

Likewise also said all the eleven disciples.

When they arrived in the gardens, Jesus said to them, Sit ye here, while I go and pray yonder." Jesus took Peter and the two sons of Zebedee with him to pray.

Salome did not want to be sent back to the women, and it was easy enough to step off the path to remain completely hidden in the darkness. She followed the four men deeper among the dark tree shadows.

Salome listened as Jesus told the three, "My soul is exceeding sorrowful, even unto death: tarry ye here, and watch with me." And he went a little farther into the garden and fell on his face, and prayed, saying, "O my Father, if it be possible, let this cup pass from me: nevertheless not as I will, but as thou wilt."

He returned to where the three disciples were and found them asleep. He said to Peter, "What, could ye not watch with me one hour? Watch and pray, that ye enter not into temptation:

the spirit indeed is willing, but the flesh is weak." He went away again the second time, and prayed, "O my Father, if this cup may not pass away from me, except I drink it, thy will be done." And He came and found them asleep again: for their eyes were heavy. And He left them, and went away again and prayed the third time, saying His same prayer.

Then He came to His disciples and said, "Sleep on now, and take your rest: behold, the hour is at hand, and the Son of man is betrayed into the hands of sinners. Rise, let us be going: behold, he is at hand that doth betray me."

And while He was yet speaking, Salome saw Judas come and with him a great sinister multitude with lanterns and torches, swords and staves, who had been gathered by the chief priests and elders of the people. Salome recognized Decius and Sextus among the soldiers. Her fear lessened somewhat, because she was confident the two Romans, who loved the Lord, would find a way to rescue Him from the mob the priests had assembled.

Judas, whose red robe appeared black in the darkness, came up to Jesus and said, "Hail, master." And he kissed Jesus.

Jesus said unto him, "Friend, wherefore art thou come?"

Then they came and laid hands on Jesus to take Him as their prisoner. So, Peter stretched out his hand and drew his sword and struck one of the Roman guards and smote off his ear.

In the melee, Salome recognized Decius when a torch illuminated his bloodied face. As if turned to unmovable stone, she watched as Jesus approached Decius and placed His hand over the wound. When He removed His hand, Decius ear was restored.

Salome pushed through the crowd to get to her husband, but was knocked down and hit the back of her head on a sharp rock.

All the torches were extinguished; but she heard Jesus say, "Put up again thy sword into his place: for all they that take the sword shall perish with the sword. Thinkest thou that I cannot now pray to my Father, and he shall presently give me more than twelve legions of angels? But how then shall the scriptures be fulfilled, that thus it must be?"

Salome wondered why no one relit their torches for the night was very dark. No one helped her up.

Jesus spoke to the noisy crowd, "Are ye come out as against a thief with swords and staves for to take me? I sat daily with you teaching in the temple and ye laid no hold on me. But all this was done, that the scriptures of the prophets might be fulfilled."

Sextus and Decius lifted Salome to her feet. "Light your torch, Decius," Salome said. "I want to see your wound again."

She heard Sextus gasp. Decius held her face close to his, then a warmth washed past her. "Salome, the torch is lit. You cannot see."

Salome reached for the place on the back of her head, where her she had struck the rock. There was no swelling, no blood. "I hit my head on a rock," she said. "Am I blind?"

Sextus's voice tried to comfort her. "It may pass, Salome."

She could hear Decius sobbing. Salome reached out her hand and he brought his wet face for her to touch. "Sextus is probably right, Decius. Take me back to Mary. Where are the apostles? Did they arrest them, too?"

Sextus said. "They were only interested in seizing our master."

As Salome stumbled along, holding onto Decius's arm, she wondered about their future. Her eyes would no longer see the sand-colored buildings and the rough walls of Palestine, she would only be able to smell the flower-bordered fields, hear the gentle flow of the Jordan, no sunsets or sunrises would mark her days, the beauty of the faces of those she loved, the ugliness

of those who hated her were lost, surely not forever. Would they need to escape to Egypt as Mary

and Joseph had after Jesus was born? If the Lord's followers left Palestine, who would comfort

the poor, the abandoned, and the sick who Jesus loved. Perhaps if they traveled all the way to

Alexandria, Mary would find someone else to help her hear the holy words of the Torah. Need

they flee so far away from Palestine to be safe from the priests and her own royal family?

                              *   *   *

                                                        The Way of the Cross

        After Sextus and Decius returned Salome to Joseph of Arimathea's house to be nursed by

Mary, they went to the High Priest's home to attend Jesus's trial. "We might yet have a chance to

free him," Decius told Sextus. But Decius felt a strange peace calming him. He had anticipated

all his warrior instincts would be heating his blood to rescue Jesus yet a deep serenity hadn't

departed since Jesus touched his severed ear.

        The Lord's words repeated again and again in his mind, "All that take the sword shall

perish with the sword."

        Decius and Sextus came upon Peter sitting in the courtyard with the high priest's

servants. The scribes and elders were assembled in the same hall where Sextus and Decius had

heard Joseph of Arimathea defend the Lord.

        Many witnesses had been paid to testify against the Lord, but when they faced Jesus, most

of them could not speak against Him. Finally one of two false witnesses spoke, "This fellow said,

I am able to destroy the temple of God, and to build it in three days."

Caiaphus rose and asked, "Answerest thou nothing? What is it which these witness against thee?" But Jesus held his peace. And the high priest said, "I adjure thee by the living God, that thou tell us whether thou be the Christ, the Son of God."

Jesus said to him, "If I tell you, ye will not believe: And if I also ask you, ye will not answer me, nor let me go. Hereafter shall ye see the Son of man sitting on the right hand of power, and coming in the clouds of heaven."

Caiaphus asked, "Art thou then the Son of God?"

Jesus answered, "Ye say I am.

And Caiaphus rent his clothing saying, "He that spoken blasphemy; what further need have we of witnesses? Behold, now ye have heard his blasphemy. What think ye?"

They answered in unison, "He is guilty of death." And they went up to the Lord and spit in his face and buffeted him and smote him with the palms of their hands, saying, "Prophesy unto us, thou Christ, Who is he that smote thee?"

Decius followed Sextus out into the fresh air.

Peter still sat in the courtyard and Decius watched as a maid approached Peter saying, "Thou also wast with Jesus in Galilee."

But Peter denied it saying, "I know not what thou sayest."

And Peter moved out onto the porch to avoid the girl, a different servant girl saw him and said to the others, "This fellow was also with Jesus of Nazareth."

Peter grunted an oath and said, "I do not know the man."

But those who stood by and had heard Peter asked again, "Surely thou also art one of them, for thy speech betrayeth thee."

Then Peter cursed loudly saying, "I know not the man." And immediately the cock

crowed. Then Peter remembered Jesus's love for him and left, crying bitterly.

*   *   *

That very morning, after agreeing in counsel to put Jesus to death the priests had Him

bound and asked two Romans, Sextus and Decius, to deliver Him to Pontius Pilate. An entire

crowd of noisy fanatics followed them. Decius had to shout to be heard on the other side of

Jesus. "We'll never be able to slip away with Him." Sextus hung his head, fully aware of their

predicament.

They escorted Him through the southernmost gate, the Essene Gate. Jesus didn't speak

but looked around Him as the torches of the crowd lit their way north around Jerusalem's wall.

He stared up at the three towers at the corner of the upper city, near Herod's palace.

As they passed by the base of Golgotha, a withered fig tree came into view. Hanging from

its strongest limb a body hung, with a red cloak still on its shoulders.

"It's Judas Iscariot," Sextus said.

Decius remembered the Lord's words, "It would have been better had he never been

born."

Decius heard the priests, who were following close behind them, say amongst themselves.

"It is not lawful for us to put the silver into the treasury, because it is the price of blood." Another

said, "We could buy a potter's field to bury strangers in with the tainted money."

Decius and Sextus could have taken their prisoner through the Fish Gate, but Decius

hoped against hope that the apostles, John the Baptist's disciples, or the rabbi's followers would have time to rescue Him from the clamoring mob behind them. The Sheep Gate on the

northeastern corner of Jerusalem was closest to the Antonia Fortress, so the priests did not object.

The four corner turrets rose above them, but no one came to save the Savior.

Hostile crowds grew in the courtyards and along the colonnades. Decius recognized Jews

from the desert draped in camel hides and lion skins, men of Galilee in working garb of

sackcloth, rich people with gold rings and gold stripes on their mantles of fine dyed linen. Jews

of Alyssinia and of Alexandria wore woolen and rough sheepskin garments. Jews from Babylon,

and Jews from the Rhine could be recognized by their heavy head coverings of wild skins. More

people were gathering in the court of the Gentiles between the rows of the columned arcade,

along the wall of the inner temple and on the countless balconies on the labyrinth of buildings

toward the fourteen rows of marble steps barring approach to the temple. Legionaries drew their

broadswords outside the Hall of Judgment. There was no direction of escape. Decius heard no

birds singing on this last morning of the Lord's.

Inside, at the governor's seat of judgment, Pilate asked Jesus, "Art thou the King of the

Jews?"

Jesus answered, "Sayest thou this thing of thyself, or did others tell it thee of me?"

Pilate answered, "Am I a Jew? Thine own nation and the chief priests have delivered thee

unto me: what hast thou done?"

Decius wondered if the Lord was fooled into believing Pilate might save Him from the

hatred of the priests.

Jesus said, "My kingdom is not of this world: if my kingdom were of this world, then

would my servants fight, that I should not be delivered to the Jews: but now is my kingdom not

from hence."

Pilate asked, "Art thou a king then?"

Jesus answered, "Thou sayest that I am a king. To this end was I born, and for this cause came I into the world, that I should bear witness unto the truth. Every one that is of the truth heareth my voice."

"What is truth?" Pilate asked.

Then Decius and Sextus heard the priests list the crimes against the Lord, again. Pilate said to Jesus, "Hearest thou not how many things they witness against thee?" And He answered him never a word. And again Pilate baited Him, "Speakest thou not to me? Knowest thou not that I have power to crucify thee, and have power to release thee?"

Jesus said, "Thou couldest have no power at all against me, except it were given thee from above: therefore he that delivered me unto thee hath the greater sin."

So Pilate brought the accused onto the balcony outside and said to the hoards of people milling about, "I find no fault at all. But ye have a custom, that I release unto you one at the Passover: will ye therefore that I release unto you the King of the Jews? Whom will ye that I release unto you? Barabbas or Jesus, who is called Christ?"

They cried, "Barabbas."

Pilate then asked them, "What shall I do then with Jesus which is called Christ?"

And they all shouted, "Let Him be crucified."

Still Pilate tried to reason with them, "Why? What evil hath He done?"

But they cried out in one voice, "Let Him be crucified."

Pilate saw that reason could not prevail against the mob. So he called his servant to bring water and Pilate washed his hands before them saying, "I am innocent of the blood of this just person: see ye to it."

Chapter Thirteen

"O Jerusalem Jerusalem, thou killest the prophets, and
stonest them which are sent unto thee, how often would I
have gathered thy children together, even as a hen gathereth
her chickens under her wings, and ye would not!"

(Is 49:5; Matt 23:37)

Sextus and Decius were relieved of their duties. Jesus was given over to the torturer to be
scourged. Sextus and Decius were torn between returning to give the news to Mary or to stay
with Jesus. Sextus took on the burden of telling Mary and the women, while Decius was left to
watch as the drunken soldiers removed Jesus's clothing.

They put a scarlet robe on Him and placed a crown of thorns on His head and a reed in
His right hand: and they bowed their knees before Him, and mocked Him, saying "Hail, King of
the Jews!" And they spit on Him and took the reed and smote Him on the head. Then they took
off the purple cape and dressed Him in His own seamless robe and led Him away to be crucified.

Decius followed as the soldiers hefted a cross to Jesus's shoulder. The tail end of the
cross bounced along the cobblestones on the way to Skull Mountain.

Jesus fell under its weight.

Decius demanded a man standing along the path help Jesus bear the weight of the cross
by carrying the end of it.

Decius staggered with the realization his gentle rabbi, who taught others to continually

forgive each other, to refrain from judging others, and to resist returning injury for injury was

denounced by His own religious leaders. Decius turned his face away from the suffering of Jesus

as the Lord painfully hauled His burden. Then Decius recognized Salome in the crowd of

onlookers.

*   *   *

When Sextus brought the news that Jesus had been condemned to crucifixion, Mary

insisted she follow her son to Golgotha. Salome begged to be taken along even though she

couldn't see; she couldn't bear to be left behind, when Mary was suffering for her son. Mary

wrapped a scarf around Salome's arm and together they trailed the noise of the crowd who were

following the Lord.

Salome heard Decius demand someone pick up the end of the cross. Mary's weeping

broke her heart. Condemned men were tortured nearly to the point of death, before the final act

of hanging them from the cross and Mary surely saw evidence of the torment. Salome joined in

with Magdalen and the other women wailing for the Lord.

Mary tugged on her wrist and Jesus's voice was very close to them. "Daughters of

Jerusalem, weep not for me, but weep for yourselves, and for your children."

Then there was a gasp from the crowd as Jesus fell to the pavement.

Magdalen touched Salome's shoulder. "I know Veronica, the woman who gave her veil to

wash the Lord's bloodied face."

Salome was glad she was blind and could not see what her countrymen had done to this gentle

rabbi. The condemned-man's procession to Golgotha wove through the poorer sections of

Jerusalem. Their rulers from Rome purposefully demonstrated to the hordes of Jewish rabble the

exact consequences metered out to rebellious leaders and prophets, who preached against them.

The lanes were narrow and steep. Market merchandise spilled out into the lanes in

baskets and from tables. The rough stone steps were uneven and broken. At many places the

street wove under the arches of houses built across the narrow way.

Women trying to follow Jesus, called out to each other when they couldn't advance

quickly enough. They attempted to find stairs around some of the obstacles, only to be left behind

on dead-end balconies, or roof tops without proper descents. At other points, Salome could hear

women running ahead, down alleys and byways, still crying to each other, trying to find their

way. Their high-pitched voices bounced off the buildings' walls along the constricted lanes

leading to Skull Mountain, called Golgotha.

Salome stretched out her arm not tied to Mary's wrist and felt the cold wall near her

shoulder. She gauged her progress down the converging lanes and up sharp turns by the sharp

ending cries of merchants barking out their wares who were silenced by the horrible sight of the

tortured, condemned prophet's last trek.

The jubilant taunts of avenging crowd of religious fanatics contrasted with the low moans

of weeping women trailing behind Mary. Salome skinned the palm of her right hand after a

gigantic step up tumbled her into the side of the rough stone wall. Mary's attention was fixed on

her suffering son's progress. Magdalen tried to steady the blinded Salome as she continued to

stumble along the uneven path. Salome could feel years being added to her life with each step.

As she touched a final section of wall warmed by the afternoon sun, she wondered if she would ever see beauty in the world again. Stabbed by guilt by this selfish thought, she asked God for

forgiveness. The Lord was not only losing the sight of the sun, His life was being taken away for

His belief.

Jesus was not as close to Mary and her, but Salome heard Him say, "For, behold, the days

are coming, in which they shall say, Blessed are the barren, and the wombs that never bear, and

the paps which never gave suck. Then shall they begin to say to the mountains, fall on us; and to

the hills, cover us. For if they do these things in a green tree, what shall be done in the dry?"

Salome put Mary's arm around her shoulder to help the stricken woman continue walking

behind her son. Even blind, the pleasures of life were still possible for Salome...not so for the

Lord. Surely He loved life as much as she did. No wonder He had prayed for His Father in

heaven to take away this burden of His ordeal.

As Mary and Decius had warned her, the Lord knew He would die for His cause. As she

continued to stagger along the way, Salome wished she had paid closer attention to the Jesus

during His brief mission. Had she known three short years would be the length of the days she

could know Him on earth, would she have attended to Him more closely?

Jesus fell a third time before they reached the city's gate to climb the hill to Skull

Mountain. Salome heard the Lord groan as He struggled to regain footing and lift His burden.

And what would His personal followers do now? Were they gathering crowds of the Lord's

supporters to save His life before the crucifixion began? Listening as closely as she could in the

surrounding din, Salome heard no sound of militant tread, no rush of noise from the hoped-for

crowds of rescuers.

Instead, the trail of tears of Mary and the women became endless. Salome's feet burned

from the long, uneven hike. Her sorrow for Mary and her son and the confusion as to her whereabouts brought tears to her eyes. Where was her husband, Decius? Why hadn't he stopped the Roman guards from carrying out Pilate's orders?

Decius was a believer. Where was he now when the Lord might yet be freed? Salome thought she might stop breathing when she realized because Decius believed, as Mary did, the Lord, the Messiah, the son of God, and Savior of the Jews, Jesus, was meant as a sacrificial lamb for all the world's sins. Surely their belief wouldn't allow this absurd cruelty to come to pass. Even Abraham was relieved of killing his son to prove his live to God.

Would Herodias's sins against Salome's father be forgiven, or would Herodias need to ask for forgiveness? Salome's mind turned away from the prospect. Even now Salome wasn't free to visit her aging father because of Herod's overriding rule. Salome would need to hide away for the rest of her life. She hoped Decius would somehow at least arrange for her to see her father before he was too old to recognize her. Even now she wouldn't be able to see his face. Salome reasoned if her blindness continued life would stretch into long hours of blackness, followed by longer hours of uselessness.

And Decius? Would he soon abandon her as she had seen family members ostracized and subjected to living in the streets begging for charity from hard-hearted religious zealots who believed God punished only the wicked? Salome was thankful when Mary stopped walking, not knowing they had reached their journey's end. She could smell the fresh country air. Thunder announced a storm was gathering. Had they reached the dreaded destination? Joseph of Arimathea, Nicodemus, and John spoke to Mary.

"Where are Decius and Sextus?" Salome asked.

John answered, "They're standing by while the soldiers are stripping the Lord."

Salome pulled on Magdalen's sleeve. "Can't they do anything?" Then she heard the hammer and knew all was lost.

Chapter Fourteen

"For God so loved the world that he gave his only begotten
Son, that whosoever believeth in him should not perish, but
have everlasting life."

(John 3:16)

Golgotha

Decius wished with all his heart he could doubt the mission of Jesus. He wanted to use

his youth, his stamina, his status as a loyal Roman soldier to undo what lay before his eyes. But

nails were hammered into the Lord's wrists and feet. Decius stood transfixed, unable to look in

Salome's direction, where she stood weeping with unseeing eyes at the sound of the hammer.

One of the priests argued with Centurion Rufus about the placard they placed on the beam

above Jesus's head, which still bled from the crown of thorns pounded on His head by Pilate's

soldiers. So that all could read who passed by, the sign was written in Hebrew, Greek and Latin:

"This is Jesus the King of the Jews."

At the third hour, the cross was placed upright so that the crucifixion of the most gentle

man the world had yet known could begin. A soldier mixed vinegar with gall and myrrh, offering

it to Jesus to drink, but He refused.

Thomas and Mary were right, Decius thought. He should never have married Salome

while she hadn't yet felt the overpowering certainty he had experienced. This tortured, bleeding

and injured man hanging above him was saving the world. Soon the Lord of all, who orchestrated this horror of ultimate suffering, would accept them all as purged souls, free of their sins of will

power gone astray, free of resentments of the actions of others, able to love each other as they

loved themselves. But where were the words to transcend the fact of their bleeding Savior nailed

hand and foot to the cross while the weight of His body strangled Him. The gentle prophet, who

had comforted Decius when he first lost sight of Salome at the Dead Sean, now hung in

unbearable pain, despised by the *holy* men of the city. Suffering for all the sins of the world,

God's Son was dying before him.

How would he ever be able to explain his in-action to his wife? The very nails piercing

the Lord's flesh had cried out to Decius. Would Salome abandon him? He imagined her

judgment, because he was a Roman still able to stop this edict from being carried out. Salome

couldn't yet share his belief in the Lord's destiny to reconcile the world to His heavenly Father.

How could she *not* condemn Decius? He knew he needed her more than ever, more than life

itself.

Jesus looked down at them and said, "Father, forgive them; for they know not what they

do."

Decius felt his feet had sprouted roots into Golgotha's stony hillside. He needed to stay

where he was, but his body urged him to flee this place of retribution. Why did the Lord need His

Son to die? Why couldn't He just pour out His love without this terrible sacrifice? Did the

creator need to experience humanness before forgiveness was warranted? Decius thanked God

for Jesus, humbled by his lack of bravery in the face of Jesus's horrific experience, he wondered

if he would ever be able to meet the eyes of his father's trusted friend. Would Sextus know him

for a coward, how could Salome accept him as her husband now that she saw, or rather would

hear of his cowardice?

Decius raised his eyes to look into his Savior's face. Jesus met his gaze. Decius

experienced the Lord's comfort, peace, forgiveness and complete understanding. Decius knelt

before his king unafraid of what the legionnaires or Sextus thought. Here was glory personified,

the Hope of the world incarnate. Decius determined to find Peter, offer his services for life to

Mary, to Salome, to anyone Peter assigned him. No stone would remain unturned to find souls

who would hear of the Lord's sacrifice to redeem their souls.

*   *   *

For three hours Salome prayed for wisdom to live as she was now: blind, helpless,

without hope. She prayed to find a way to be useful to Decius. She trusted him to help in her

modest quest. Salome's blindness protected her from seeing Jesus hanging on the cross. How

would she have endured watching her son suffer such an ignominious death? Mary believed her

son was carrying out their heavenly Father's will. Nevertheless, before this very human gentle

mother, her first born son suffered before her sight.

Salome's mind searched through the teachings of Isaiah for comfort, but found only

prophesy fulfilled. Here in Jerusalem, which the prophet called "the city of righteousness, the

faithful city," Jews were crucifying a great teacher, their Messiah. Why didn't Decius or Sextus

demand that the Lord be released? Did their belief prevent them from intervention? Was her

husband able to stand by at such cruelty?

"For Jerusalem is ruined and Judah is fallen: because their tongue and their doings are

against the Lord, to provoke the eyes of His glory." And Salome remembered more of Isaiah's admonitions, "And her gates shall lament and mourn; and she being desolate shall sit upon the ground."

Mary stood as a pillar of spiritual strength, a witness to her son's suffering.

Salome wept and sat on the rocky, cold ground, untying the scarf that Mary had bound to her wrist. She knew she must not distract Mary, not now…not while there was still breath in her son's body.

Isaiah's words spelled out Salome's grief, "Woe unto them that call evil good, and good evil; that put darkness for light, and light for darkness; that put bitter for sweet, and sweet for bitter."

As the hours passed, Salome had time to review her doubts about Jesus's healings and the miracles she, Thomas and Decius witnessed firsthand. Would she be as serene as Mary, if she believed the Lord was redeeming their souls? In Cana at the wedding feast, was she certain none of water jars' contents were turned into wine? She hadn't been able to watch every servant. When Dorcas was healed after Sextus had asked to the Lord to come to Nazareth, would Dorcas had survived without the Lord's intercession?

Mostly, Salome rued the wasted days, when she was separated from Decius by his stronger belief in the Lord's mission. The woman who touched the hem of the Lord's garment, would she have been healed of her ailments without a miracle? And in Gergesenes, could evil be driven out of people? Why didn't the Lord turn the hearts of His persecutors to believe in Him? Why was she left to doubt, when all else who loved the Lord, believed He would save them all?

She had forgiven Herodias. Mary had suggested the resentment against her mother might be her only stumbling block to belief. Resentment had been a burden, but faith eluded Salome even after Herodias was forgiven. Salome's head pounded from its bruising at Gethsemane. Would she be permanently blinded from her fall?

The early spring warmth caressed her shoulders. There was no other place on earth she would rather be than here, while the Lord died on the cross, and Mary suffered. Salome acknowledged she was on holy ground.

Abraham had agreed to sacrifice Isaac, his first born, to prove his love for God. And was God sacrificing His Son because He loved the world of His creation that much?

The perfumes from Magdalen's hair wafted past Salome. Salome raised her own veil and covered her head. The pain of her firstborn's death was as real as the day she lost him. Salome felt an added burden to the extraordinarily bleak scene she was unable to witness. She was no longer angry at God for taking her son, when He might be ready to let His own Son suffer so terribly for them. Salome had covered her head to bear witness to God, humbled by His ability to love them at the expense of His only Son.

As the atmosphere of storm and defeat claimed the hill, Salome listened to the conversations of the people surrounding them. Fewer and fewer people watched or witnessed on the Mount. She remembered the terrors of the path to the mount, shivered as the winds continued to buffet them. 'Lord,' she prayed in complete silent submission, 'Your will, not mine, be done.'

She heard John and Joseph of Arimathea speak softly to Mary again, trying to persuade her to leave. Salome stood. "She must remain," she said. "We will stay with her." Mary sought out Salome's hand. Salome knelt beside her, thankful that she'd spoken Mary's wishes.

*   *   *

Cold winds began to howl on the mountain. Decius watched huge black and green storm clouds race low over their heads. The heartless soldiers cast lots for Jesus's robe because the garment was seamless, woven by Mary the mother of this holy man. Decius couldn't bear to watch the woman, whose hospitality saved Salome's life. Remaining loyal to her son, in spite of her terror and unbearable sorrow, Mary would not leave Skull Mountain.

Even while the purple clouds lowered over their heads, the rabble slung bitter words at Jesus. "Thou that destroyed the temple and buildest it in three days, save thyself."

Lightning jumped from cloud to cloud will rolls of sinister thunder. Yet, other onlookers reviled Him shouting, "If thou be the Son of God, come down from the cross."

Even the chief priests, scribes and elders of the people taunted him, "He saved others: himself he cannot save."

A green glow lit the mountain as the storm threatened to sweep the hill of every living thing. Another scribe yelled, "If he be King of Israel, let him now come down from the cross and we will believe him."

"He trusted in God; let him deliver him now," another priest tempted the heavens, "if he will have him: for he said, 'I am the Son of God.'"

Lightning began to strike close to Golgotha, thunder increased its volume, and Decius smelled the threatening rain.

*   *   *

With each syllable of cruel words thrown at the Lord, Salome cringed as if stones were pelting her. Salome's body started to shake. She refused to give into the spasms washing over her, reasoning them to be a reaction to ungrounded fears. Fear, she knew, never came from God.

Was she brave enough to question God? She wasn't that foolish, was she? Salome refused to

sound her doubts now, not while this gentle man of God was leaving the earth. Decius's words

came drifting through the painful rubble in her mind, 'for God so loved the world...'

Abraham's hand had been stayed by an angel. The hecklers were asking Jesus to call

down the angels to deliver Him. Abraham proved his love to the Lord. Was God now proving

His love of mankind, His creation, by allowing His son to be crucified? Or was Jesus the

instigator of this sacrifice? Did His mother teach Him that He was the Messiah and was destined

to save the world? Did the unearthly begetting of Jesus come with the message of His destruction

and salvation?

Salome's mind buzzed like a swarm of bees circling her head. She reached up to touch

the back of her head, no bump evident. Was she going to die the same way Ide did after she

bumped her head into the wall near Jericho? Instantly, Salome rued the self-pity she experienced,

sinning while the Lord hung before her unseeing eyes. She dared to reach out toward Mary,

touched her shoulder and experienced a shock of pain throughout her own body as she

empathized with the stricken woman. Salome again thanked God that He had blinded her against

the scene that Mary was witnessing. The Holy Mother's shoulder dipped slightly in her direction.

Tears washed down Salome's face. How could this older, sighted mother watch as the life

drained out of her son?

Were the apostles lurking near, or were they frightened by the vengeance of the Jewish

priests? Would the people of Israel be abandoned to the corrupt hawkers who called themselves

ministers to God? The Lord's gentle teachings to love each other rather than judging the purity of

ritual keeping, allowed the sick and the destitute an avenue of redemption. Loving cost no money. No doves, or goats, or sacrificial ox needed to be purchased for sacrifice. Loving God needn't shed blood. Yet here was Jesus bleeding before them, the ultimate sacrifice. And if He was the Son of God, then was He experiencing every sin, each avaricious thought, each lecherous deed, each revengeful act. How the God in Heave must love them all!

The late spring afternoon was cooling quickly with winds rising from all directions. Salome shuddered from the cold. She was thirsty and sucked her teeth to wet her tongue. The taste of blood nearly gagged her and her headache disappeared.

Her mind cleared.

A stillness came upon the hill, no birds sang. She could smell Magdalen's hair again, when a sudden stiff breeze blew her curls out from under her veil and into Salome's face. The lessening noise might mean that the angry crowds were melting away because of the travesty of justice before them, or the atmospheric, conflagration of the storm.

"Thank you Lord," Salome prayed because she could not see the carnage the mob had wreaked. Was God's plan at work here?

Isaiah's words blew upon her as the gusts of winds began to buffet her anew. "Make the heart of this people fat, and make their ears heavy, and shut their eyes' lest they see with the eyes, and hear with the ears, and understand with their heart, and convert, and be healed."

Salome tried to lay out in sequence the many passages of Isaiah which pointed in the Lord's final direction. At this late date, would she come to believe in the Lord's mission while she waited at the foot of the cross for the Lord to perish? She bravely searched her memory for certainty. "Ask thee a sign of the Lord God. Therefore Lord himself shall give you a sign: Behold a virgin shall conceive, and bear a son, and shall call his name Immanuel."

Mary's story of the birth of Jesus passed through Salome's mind. "And the spirit of the Lord shall rest upon Him, the spirit of wisdom and understanding, the spirit of counsel and might, the spirit of knowledge and of the fear of the Lord. And shall make him a quick understanding in the fear of the Lord: and he shall not judge after sight of his eyes, neither reprove after the hearing of his ears."

And where was Decius? Salome tried to listen for his voice, but no one was speaking, except for Isaiah within the confines of her mind. "The people that walked in darkness have seen a great light; they that dwell in the land of the shadow of death, upon them hath the light shined."

She no longer felt warmth from the sun. Was she destined to remain a non-believer? What would happen next? Was the very world ending? As if the sky had opened to weep, a cold rain whipped at Salome's veil and tunic.

Joseph had returned to his home and brought a warm cape for Mary. He draped another around Salome's shoulders. "Courage, little…" Salome reached out to thank him and the old man touched his forehead to her palm. "Princess," he whispered.

Why was she a blind witness to Jesus's death? What role did she play in the death of the two prophets, John the Baptist and Jesus of Nazareth? Did the Lord in Heaven deem her worthy enough to be so closely involved in the deaths of both men of God? The task of finding meaning in the events of her life confounded reason. Then she remembered a saying Thomas repeated often. "When I die I expect God will tell me the story of my life."

Her life as a young girl surrounded by privilege and servants to meet her every need, materialized as if she had lived in a different historical age, where poverty, hunger, and the elements of nature, cold and rain, were non-existent. Salome remembered watching the rain pound the terrace tiles outside her bedroom as it now pounded down on her veil-covered hair. Joseph's robe helped her bones not feel the cold her face endured.

There she was back to salving herself while those around her suffered unendurable painful sights. Would a God understand her? Would he give her daily comfort while she bore the burden of blindness? What could she contribute to the mission Jesus had set for all of them to teach others to love each other as they loved themselves? Her only gift was her ability to keep time with music to entertain a gluttonous, villain, the Tetrarch Herod. She could no longer help Mary read the Torah. What plan did God, her creator, have for her? Would she recognize her destiny? "Lord," she prayed aloud, "Thy will be done."

Magdalen embraced her, "You are here for a reason Salome. Take heart."

The next cruel gust of rain and sleet did not disturb Salome. She'd been comforted by Magdalen. Surely not knowing her future could be borne easier than Mary's endurance from the stabbing of her gentle heart, witnessing the death of her son.

Something that had never happened in the universe was happening within Salome's earshot. God was reconciling himself to his creation by undergoing all the sins that free will allowed: all the pain of regret, all the fears of abandonment, all the anger and resentment against those that injured each other. Jesus's gentle heart experienced every human emotion, every physical illness and pain, every despair, every groundless hope. Salome prayed for her own redemption, "Let me find your way, Lord."

                              *   *   *

Two thieves were crucified with Jesus, one on his right and one on his left. Decius remembered how the mother of the sons of Zebedee once asked for such positions in heaven for James and John.

One of the malefactors shouted at Jesus, "If Thou be Christ, save thyself and us."

But the other rebuked him. "Dost not thou fear God, seeing thou art in the same condemnation? We indeed, justly, for we receive the due reward of our deeds; but this man hath done nothing amiss." Then he said to Jesus, "Lord, remember me when thou comest into Thy kingdom."

And Jesus said, "Verily, I say unto thee, today shalt thou be with me in paradise."

As brutal, pelting rain began to drench everyone, Decius regained his courage and looked from Sextus to the people gathering at the foot of the cross. Salome had covered her hair with her veil. Decius had shared her grief, he knew by covering her head Salome had stopped hating God. Mary with Magdalen, John, Joseph, and Nicodemus attended the deathwatch. Most of the crowds had taken refuge from the hill while the storm continued to roar about them.

At the sixth hour, complete darkness covered the land from the vicious storm until the ninth hour. Then Jesus cried with a loud voice, "Eli, Eli, la'ma sa-bach'-tha-ni'?" That said, "My God, My God, Why hast Thou forsaken me?"

The onlookers who hadn't been discouraged by the storm said, "This man calleth for Elias."

Others said, "He said, 'I thirst.'"

Straightway one of them ran, and took a sponge, and filled it with the vinegar potion and put it on a reed, and gave him a drink.

Others cried, "Let be. Let us see whether Elias will come to save him."

When Jesus cried again with a loud voice, "Father, into Thy hands I commend my spirit," he yielded up the ghost.

*　　*　　*

The Lord's sharp final cry awakened Salome from a slight stupor. Magdalen's sigh was followed by a great roar coming from the direction of the temple behind them. People were shouting and running towards them. Their voices sounded like handfuls of pebbles being thrown into stone jars.

The news approached, then reached Skull Mountain. For behold, the veil of the temple was rent in twain from the top to the bottom.

The earth began to shake and quake and the rocks were rent apart. Salome felt the earth shift as lightning struck all around them. The thunder was deafening but she had heard the Lord's last words on earth. The winds increased. There was no way to turn with their back against the wind, because the winds were striking them from all four directions. Rocks seemed to be splitting apart on their own volition or because of the strikes from the lightning. Salome wondered if the world would end. Was God drawing His Son to Heaven and in his anger releasing a final destruction on the world?

"And He shall smite the earth with the rod of his mouth, and with the breath of his lips shall he slay the wicked." According to Isaiah, this might be the time when life would end. "Behold, the day of the Lord cometh, cruel both with wrath and fierce anger, to lay the land desolate; and he shall destroy the sinners thereof out of it."

Salome couldn't see if the sky still held above them; but Isaiah had said, "For the stars of heaven and the constellations thereof shall not give their light: the sun shall be darkened in his going forth, and the moon shall not cause her light to shine. And I will punish the world for their evil and the wicked for their iniquity, and I will cause the arrogance of the proud to cease, and will lay low the haughtiness of the terrible."

But hadn't the Lord said he hadn't come to judge but to save his people? "Therefore I shall shake the heavens, and the earth shall remove out of her place, in the wrath of the Lord of hosts, and in the day of his fierce anger."

Salome trembled in fear from the prophets remembered words. She reached out her hand for comfort.

Magdalen embraced her shoulders. "Steady, little sister. The Lord loves us, even the more now."

*   *   *

Now when the Centurion Rufus and the soldiers watching Jesus, saw the earthquake, they feared greatly, saying, "Truly, this was the Son of God."

So, Centurion Rufus took his spear and pierced the Lord's side, and forthwith came out blood and water. Then the soldiers began to break the legs of the condemned, but when they saw that Jesus was dead already, they did not break his legs.

Decius was with Joseph, when he spoke to Rufus, "Pilate has marveled that Jesus is already dead. He has given me permission to remove the body."

Joseph of Arimathea brought Mary closer to the foot of the cross where John and Nicodemus removed the body of Christ from the cross, wrapping Jesus's body in a fine linen cloth. They laid the body in Mary's lap. Nicodemus had brought a mixture of myrrh and aloes, about an hundred pound weight, to anoint the body. The women had prepared spices and ointments. The sad procession silently carried the burial litter to Joseph's own sepulcher and laid the Lord's body in the tomb that was hewn out of stone.

Soldiers followed them and rolled a stone against the door of the cave and then took up positions to stand watch. Decius heard Sextus demand to know their orders.

"The Pharisees went together to Pilate. They told him that while Jesus was still alive he'd prophesized, 'After three days, I will rise again.' The priests are afraid his followers will come in the night and steal his body and then say that he is risen from the dead."

Decius hadn't approached Salome. He prayed his wife would someday understand and forgive him because of his role in the crucifixion of Jesus. Decius was without hope that she could ever understand, yet he trusted in the Lord.

Magdalen sought him out on the path back to Joseph's home. "Decius, do not weep, and do not grieve, and do not doubt; for His grace will be with us completely, and He will protect us."

*   *   *

The first night without the Lord, Nathaniel joined Joseph's table with the eleven apostles. The women were indisposed by their grief, so Janus, Simon and Jude served leftover food from the Passover. Decius and Sextus stood watch at the doors.

Magdalen came and sat where Jesus had eaten his last meal. She rose and addressed the somber assembly. "We experienced Christ's presence in the present. Those who come after will encounter Christ first on the level of inner experience." Magdalen looked at the silent crowd and returned to the kitchen.

Thomas took his turn at rallying the grief-stricken men. "Jesus told me, 'If you bring forth what is within you, what you bring forth will save you. If you do not bring forth what is within you, what you do not bring forth will destroy you."

"He is our guide," Joseph said, "to open access to spiritual understanding."

Thomas frowned, muttering, "Are you saying God is only a matter of focus?"

Peter, who had not touched his food, spoke. "Jesus was not our master. Because we have drunk of his suffering, we have become drunk from the bubbling stream which he has measured out...of grace. Those who will drink of it will become saved."

Andrew re-entered the hall. "I've spoken to Mary," he said. "She has a message for us."

Mary opened the door to the kitchen, where the women were now eating.

Decius could smell the soup bubbling on the stove. Could they use rose petals as a spice? Salome was eating a piece of bread. He smiled at her before he remembered she couldn't see. Her green eyes shone with unshed tears. Magdalen was braiding, Salome's long curls, as if to help her better groom her soft hair. Decius still feared his wife's reproach. He felt he would not be able to sustain such a blow while the sights of Golgotha remained in the forefront of his brain, vividly replaying the horror of the Lord's death. He imagined still hearing the hammer pound nails into the Lord's flesh. Salome's rejection would kill him, he was sure. He looked at the untouched salted fish in his plate. Would he ever be able to take nourishment again?

Mary stepped into the dining hall. "The things that are hidden will be revealed," she said. "Jesus once told me, 'If spirit came into being because of the body, it is a wonder of wonders.

Indeed, I am amazed at how this great wealth (the spirit) has made its home in this poverty of the body.'"

John spoke up, "Remember when I told the Lord, 'We do not know where you are going, how can we know the way?' Jesus said, 'I am the way, the truth, and the life, no one comes to the Father, but by me.'"

James stood next to John. "Look, if people say the Kingdom is in the sky, the birds will arrive before us."

Philip took up the refrain, "If they say to you, 'It is in the sea,' then the fish will arrive before you."

Bartholomew instructed Matthew, "Write this down, the Kingdom of Heaven is a state of inner discovery...never perfected."

Decius was heartened by their words. He bravely entered the kitchen and knelt next to Salome. "Have you listened to the apostles?" Salome nodded. "Forgive me," Decius said. "The Kingdom is inside of you, and it is outside of you. When you come to know yourself, then you will be known, and you will realize that you are the child of the living Father. But if you will not know yourself, then you dwell in poverty, and it is you who are that poverty."

Decius's heart still knew the peace he'd accepted at Golgotha. He held Salome close to him that night as she slept, hearing the moans of her night terrors. He prayed for the recovery of her sight but dedicated himself to serving her every need.

Chapter Fifteen

"Thus it is written, and thus it behoved Christ to
suffer, and to rise from the dead the third day."
(Hos 6:1-2; Luke 24:46)

Jerusalem

Salome cried herself to sleep, unable to dislodge the word 'poverty' from her thoughts. In her dreams she walked among the sumptuous, lavish halls of Herod's palace in Jerusalem. Each opulent room was decorated with the most luxurious red draperies and gold-inlaid furniture. Salome lit a scented candle to help her find her sleeping room among the deserted chambers. She noticed her fingernails were bitten to the quick. Her mouth tasted of blood. Curls lying on her shoulder turned to red snakes.

She woke to the sound of spring birds warbling at the rising sun. Salome rubbed matting from her sightless eyes. She remembered words from Isaiah, "Arise, shine, for the light is come and the glory of the Lord is risen upon them." She could almost hear the Lord's words, "I am the good shepherd and know my sheep and am known of mine."

Decius rolled toward her in the marital bed. She felt him jump from the bed. "Your eyes are bleeding!"

Mary and Magdalen were summoned and came with soft warm clothes to wash her face. Mary's voice soothed her fears. "The pressure has probably been released."

"Will her sight return?" Magdalen asked.

"Salome," Mary said, "We can only pray that it does."

Magdalen said, "Decius, will you stay with her? We're visiting the Lord's sepulcher with more ointments this morning."

"Who will roll the stone away for you," Salome asked, "if Decius stays with me? Have my eyes stopped bleeding? Let me come with you."

*   *   *

Decius let Salome use his arm for their trip to the Lord's tomb.

Magdalen spoke all the way to the tomb. "I can't believe that I will never see Him on this earth again. How could He leave us so early in His life?"

Salome tried to hush Magdalen, to save Mary's feelings.

"We will miss Him," Mary said. "He told me when He was just a boy and we had lost Him in the pilgrimage crowds for Passover that He had to be about His father's business. The Lord will always be alive in our hearts. While we yet live, Christ lives."

"Will we be all right?" Magdalen asked.

"He promised," Mary said.

"I won't be needed to roll the stone away," Decius said. "The entrance of the tomb is open."

Salome asked, "Decius, would the soldiers have desecrated the Lord's body?"

Magdalen and Mary entered the tomb.

When they came out, Salome saw their faces were shining with happiness.

"He's not here," Magdalen cried out.

"Jesus has risen," Mary, his holy mother declared. "He goes before us into Galilee. Christ said to me, 'Touch me not; for I am not ascended to my Father: but go to my brethren, and say unto them, I ascend unto my Father, and your Father; and to my God and your God.'"

*   *   *

Magdalen was the first to reach Decius. "Salome's sight has been restored!"

"Praise the Lord." Decius embraced the former harlot, forgetting any social barrier. Salome approached them while Decius still had his arms around Magdalen. But Salome smiled directly at him, held her arms out in welcome. He rushed across the short distance between them. Decius kissed her face, her eyes, her mouth. "Salome." He didn't recognize his own emotion-packed voice.

She pushed him away and looked directly into his eyes. "The Lord has risen, Decius. God has restored his temple in all of us."

"You believe," Decius said, wondering if his heart would burst with happiness.

Salome knelt when Decius did. She asked Mary, "Will my heart break with joy?"

"No," Mary said. "Even though the entire world now shouts with joy for all of us redeemed by the grace of Christ, you will live forever in his love."

And they hurried to tell the apostles that Christ had risen.

Chapter Sixteen

"Go ye into all the world, and preach the gospel to
every creature. He that believeth and is baptized
shall be saved; but he that believeth not shall be
damned."

(Matt 28:19; Mark 16:15-16)

Sea of Galilee

Decius joined some of the apostles as they put to sea. They caught no fish. And when they

were in the midst of the sea, a great tempest immediately arose, covering the small boat with

waves. And in the fourth watch of the night, Christ went unto them, walking on the sea.

And when the disciples saw Him walking on the sea, they were troubled saying, "It is a

spirit!" and they cried out for fear.

But straightaway Christ spoke unto them, saying, "Be of good cheer; it is I; be not afraid."

And Peter answered him and said, Lord, if it be thou, bid me come unto thee on the

water."

And He said, "Come."

And when Peter was come down out of the boat, he walked on the water, to go to Christ.

But when he saw the wind boisterous, he was afraid; and beginning to sink, he cried, saying,

"Lord, save me."

"And immediately Christ stretched forth his hand and caught him and said unto him, "O thou of little faith, wherefore didst thou doubt?"

And when they came into the ship, the wind ceased.

Christ said to them, "All power is given unto me in heaven and in earth. Go ye therefore, and teach all nations, baptizing them in the name of the Father and of the Son, and of the Holy Ghost: Teaching them to observe all things whatsoever I have commanded you, and lo, I am with you always, even unto the end of the world."

* * *

Capernaum

Salome found Thomas weeping outside the dining room. She wiped his tears away with her hair. "What is it?"

Thomas pointed to her husband. "Even Decius has seen the risen Christ." He hung his head in pain. "Except I shall see in his hands the print of the nails, and put my finger into the print of the nails, and thrust my hand into his side, I will not believe."

Salome said, "You know that I no longer doubt the Lord?"

"You saw his empty tomb on the third day?"

"I'm not sure," Salome said. "I had been blind and two days may have passed." She followed Decius and Thomas into the dining room.

Christ stood before them, and he said to Thomas, "Reach hither thy finger, and behold my hands: and reach hither thy hand, and thrust it into my side: and be not faithless, but believing."

Thomas answered, "My Lord and My God."

Christ said, "Thomas, because thou hast seen me, thou hast believed: blessed are they that have not seen and yet have believed."

Then he turned to the apostles and said, Peace be unto you: as my Father hath sent me, even so send I you. Receive ye the Holy Ghost: Whosoever sins ye remit, they are remitted unto them; and whose so ever sins ye retain, they are retrained."

And Christ said to Salome, "Have ye here any meat?" And she gave him a piece of a broiled fish and of an honey comb. And He took it and did eat before them all. And Christ said unto them, "These are the words which I spake unto you, while I was yet with you, that all things must be fulfilled, which were written in the law of Moses, and in the prophets and in the psalms concerning me. Thus it is written, and thus it behoved Christ to suffer, and to rise from the dead the third day: and that repentance and remission of sins should be preached in his name among all nations, beginning at Jerusalem. And ye are witnesses of these things. And, behold, I send the promise of my Father upon you; but tarry ye in the city of Jerusalem, until ye be endued with power from on high."

And when He had parted from them, Salome understood the story of Abraham and Isaac for the first time. Of course, a human could not redeem the world by offering his only son to prove his love for God.

God needed to offer His only son so that He might reclaim the souls of those He created. God so loved the world!

*   *   *

Nazareth, Heshuan (Oct) 31 AD

More than a year later, at the dinner table in his Nazareth home, Decius listened to John and Matthew arguing. Today the topic was whether John the Baptist was still alive after Jesus drove the moneylenders out of the temple, when they had accompanied Jesus to Jerusalem for their first Passover together.

John said, "John the Baptist and Jesus's disciples were baptizing people in Aenon near to Salem after the first Passover."

After checking his notes, Matthew disagreed.

Decius settled the controversy. "I was at Machaerus when John the Baptist was killed before Jesus's first miracle in Cana.

"It doesn't matter." Matthew said, "The important message is salvation for all believers."

John was about to continue the argument when there was a knock at the door.

Decius excused himself, because Salome was in their bed chamber resting after nursing their twin sons.

An old woman stood on the doorstep. "Is this Salome's home?"

"Yes," Decius said, offering an arm to the woman who seemed about to fall down in exhaustion. "Come in. Sit down, please. Matthew, please bring water for my guest."

"I'm Lydia," the woman said. "Herodias…." The fragile woman fainted.

Decius picked her up and carried her into Salome. He placed her on the bed next to Salome, then gently woke his wife. "Your mother's old servant has sought you out."

"Lydia?" Salome asked, rolling over look at the woman. "Take the boys," she said handing first one and then the other of the twins to Decius. "Your guests can hold them while I find out what brings Lydia all this way."

Decius managed to hold both infants securely. When he reached the dining room, he bent

over Matthew. "This is Samuel, I think. Just hold him for me. Salome's busy."

To John, Decius said, "Here, take Jason. They'll both keep sleeping, if we talk softly. No

arguing."

*   *   *

Salome brought a chair to the side of the bed where Lydia slept. She thought about letting

her rest, but her curiosity caused her to wake the woman. "Please, Lydia. What news?"

Lydia tried to rise, but Salome held her shoulder down. "Salome. I finally told your

mother you forgave her after one of your father Philip's servants let it be known that he had

approved a marriage between you and a Roman guard. Was that Decius Invictus that opened the

door? Herodias has banished me. I'm lucky to be alive. Her wrath knows no bounds."

Salome could imagine the scene. "Your home is here now. Sleep. We'll talk after you've

rested." Lydia instantly closed her eyes from fatigue.

Decius re-entered the room. Salome hushed him and they used the door to the garden,

devoid of blooms, for a private talk. "Is Herodias ill?" Decius asked.

"No," Salome said, shaking her head. "Just up to her old evilness. Lydia will be staying

with us now."

"We'll need to move to a bigger place for the boys." Decius drew Salome to him,

wrapped his cloak around her shoulders. "It's too cold out here."

Salome whispered to him, "We must flee as Mary and Joseph fled after the birth of

Christ."

"Why are you afraid?" Decius asked. "Your mother won't dare harm you. The Jews in power are happy that they have killed the Lord."

"No one is happy with us, Decius." Salome went into the main room where the apostles, Mathew and John held her boys, Jason and Samuel.

Matthew handed Samuel back to Salome and agreed with her. "Peter's nephew, Stephen, was not allowed in the synagogue yesterday."

"Because he is not from Nazareth?" Decius tried to comprehend the intricacies of the Jewish religion, but every rule had two conditions. "Here, I'll take him now," Decius took his son, Jason, from John.

"No." Salome sat at the table. "Stephen was seen speaking to me. They know that I believe the Lord is the Messiah."

"They will not allow followers of the rabbi into their synagogue?" Decius believed his wife but the reasoning behind their dismissal of a fellow Jew seemed vague.

"And Mary." Salome swallowed a sob. "They will not allow us to clean the synagogue, so I can't read the Torah to Mary anymore."

"Does Mary want to leave Nazareth?" Matthew asked.

"I think she does," Salome said.

*   *   *

Jerusalem

The apostles met with their growing group of refugees in Joseph's house in Jerusalem. Salome remembered the Lord's last supper in the room. Now a year and a half after his death, his followers were being persecuted for their belief in his salvation.

After breaking bread with the assembled in remembrance of the Lord, Decius spoke to the

elders. "I can no longer accept payment as an occupier of your people. Salome and I do not wish

to raise our children as pagans in Rome. We're no longer welcome in Nazareth. Mary believes

Egypt will be a safe place, as it was where she and her husband, Joseph, fled with their son,

Jesus."

Thomas stood. "I'm leaving for India. I want to find the family of the royal visitor of

Magdalen's in Magdala. I believe I'll discover the people there have a natural capacity to love the

Lord. I have no home in Palestine."

Peter was helped to stand by his nephew, Stephen. "I believe Rome will be converted.

Perhaps not in my lifetime, but surely before the next generation passes. Is anyone willing to

travel with me?"

Salome gasped as Sextus stood. "Dorcas and I plan to follow Holy Mother Mary and my

charge, Decius' family into Egypt. Alexandria contains a library which houses copies of the

Torah. Even if the Jews do not allow us into their synagogues, we will have access to the words

of God."

Mary spoke softly, but everyone gave their rapt attention. "Matthew, my doctor Luke, our

friend Mark and John, here, are all making written records in Greek of our Lord's teachings.

When Peter builds a congregation in Rome, make sure they receive copies. I believe Jerusalem

will be beaten down to ash, soon. Take copies of the Lord's teachings to the Essenes in the hills

beyond the Dead Sea. They will protect them there."

Decius told the group, "I will be able to be employed in Alexandria. Sextus has family

there, too. Magdalen no longer wants to stay in Palestine, either. Will any of the rest of you want

to join us?"